RUMOR

A RENEGADES NOVEL

SKYE JORDAN

1

This had been an epically stupid idea.

Josh Marx propped his elbows on the picnic table, flanking his laptop, and stared out at the ocean beyond Dana Point Harbor, in California. With a storm brewing, the general public had deserted the beach, and only a small group of his friends from the Renegades Stunt Company wandered down by the water's edge.

On the beach, Jax Chamberlin, the owner of Renegades, rocketed a football through the air toward Wes Lawson, Renegades' top stunt driver. The wind hooked the ball five yards inland, and Wes launched off his feet, stretching until he was horizontal to the sand, arms extending, stretching, reaching...

The ball brushed his fingertips and changed trajectory, spinning away as Wes dove—face-first—into the sand.

The others broke into hysterics. Wes pushed to hands and knees, shook sand out of his hair, and spit it out of his mouth. Josh chuckled but the heaviness in his chest clung.

Rubi, Wes's girlfriend, jogged up the beach, grabbed a towel, and tossed it to Wes, then wandered toward the picnic table. She darted a look at the notepad at Josh's elbow, where he'd jotted calculations.

"Done yet?"

"Not even close." Josh returned his gaze to the sea, a bitter-sweet knot forming beneath his ribs. "I figured if I stall long enough, you'll have that risk assessment app all finished, and I wouldn't have to do anything but plug in numbers."

"Can't create it without your help." The computer savant eyed him across the table. "When's that going to happen, anyway?"

Josh heaved a breath and rubbed the backs of his fingers against the stubble on his jaw. He'd been so busy with different consulting gigs, he hadn't had time to sit down with Rubi and give her the information she needed to program the application. "How about right after Christmas? I'll have a few days free between seeing my parents and starting another job."

"You're on."

Wes and Jax were tossing the ball again.

"No!" Rachel's scream drew Josh's gaze to the waterline just as Ryker hoisted her over his shoulder and waded into the surf. "Nathan, don't you *dare*. That water's freezing."

A half smile curled Josh's mouth. He'd spent twelve-hour days training in that sixty-degree water during BUDS. His thoughts circled back to the loss of his career and the life he loved. Over the past twelve months, emptiness continued to haunt him, contrary to the navy therapist's promise that it would dissipate with time.

He loved a broody ocean, and now, the southern California sky hung heavy with storm clouds, making the water an intense shade of steel blue. The two-hundred-foot tall eucalyptus over-head rattled in the growing wind. White caps developed a mile offshore.

God, it was all so perfect. So beautiful. And made him so damned lonely.

"Want to talk about it?" Rubi asked.

Josh dragged his gaze away from the group and the ocean beyond, refocusing on the screen where risk assessment forms stared back at him. "Nah. It won't take me long to get this written up when I'm not distracted."

"I meant"—Rubi's words pulled his gaze from the water— "whatever's bugging you?"

To avoid her piercing eyes, Josh glanced back at the screen just as a handful of raindrops slanted across the glass. He shut his laptop and stuffed his things back into his briefcase. "Is there something bugging me?"

"You've definitely been out of sorts the last couple of days. Withdrawn, quiet... Dare I say...moody?"

"Have I?"

"It's Rachel and Ryker, isn't it?"

More of Rachel's screaming laughter floated on the wind, and he smiled. He'd missed her since she'd moved to Virginia and shacked up with army boy. But he didn't miss her like he'd expected to miss someone he'd been in love with. He just missed her like he missed other friends who'd come and gone from his shifting life. Which confirmed that he hadn't been in love with Rachel at all. Just wishing he could have been, because falling for someone else could have erased the one woman he'd wanted for years from his heart and mind.

"No, it's not them. I just still have a lot to do before I head home."

What Rubi sensed was that nagging emptiness cresting on this significant date, making him remember all he'd lost. Making him realize how deeply he craved someone permanent beside him. Someone intimately in tune with who he was, what he believed in, and how he thought. Outside his team, there was only one woman in the world who understood him that way—and it wasn't Rachel.

To keep his mind from straying to Grace, he let it drift to his team. To where they might be now—Syria, Iraq, Afghanistan, Asia. To what journalist they'd been dispatched to rescue. What diplomat they might be protecting. What guerrilla military group they'd been ordered to dismantle...

"Heads up!" someone yelled from the beach.

Josh looked over as the football sailed toward them. In split-second intervals, he calculated the trajectory, pushed to his feet, and dove across the table, intercepting the ball inches from Rubi's face. The ball slammed into his outstretched hand, torquing his shoulder. Pain knifed down his arm, up his neck, and across his chest. Burning, shooting, fiery stabbing pain.

"*Motherfucker*—" He fell against the table and clenched his teeth against the pain. "That boyfriend of yours has a good arm."

"And you've got some good moves," Rubi said, standing now, her hand lying gently on his back. "Are you all right?"

Some days, he felt like a fucking cripple. "Will be, thanks."

He straightened, barely stemming a wince at the slice along his shoulder.

Wes jogged toward the table, sand still clinging to his T-shirt, a frown of concern pulling his brow. He hooked an arm around Rubi's shoulders, wrapped a hand around the back of her neck, and pulled her forehead to his. "God, I'm sorry, baby."

"You got lucky," she said, grinning. "Marx saved you from a dire fate."

Wes brushed his fingers across her cheek, staring into her eyes, but spoke to Josh. "Thanks for saving this beautiful face, man."

And he kissed her. Passionately.

That was the last straw for Josh. He was happy for all the love in his friends' lives. First Jax and Lexi, then Wes and Rubi. Now Rachel and Ryker. He wasn't envious of what they'd all found, not really, but the constant reminder of what he didn't have wore on his nerves.

He picked up his briefcase and slid his other hand into the pocket of his slacks to take the weight off his shoulder. "I'm gonna hit the road."

Wes and Rubi broke from their kiss, and Wes glanced his way. "Leaving already?"

"I'm not getting anything done here."

"Dude," Wes said, pulling Rubi in front of him and slipping his arms around her waist, "it's *Sunday*. Get out of those work rags and take a few laps in the waves. You need to learn how to relax."

Agreed. He sucked at relaxing. But his younger brothers always beat Josh's ingrained conservatism away within a day of meeting up. And it had been far too long since the three of them had spent any quality time together. The thought of heading home for Christmas really turned his mood around. This was exactly what he needed.

"I'm headed that direction right now. Tell Jax I'll e-mail the assessment as soon as I'm done, but I don't see any problems."

Josh turned for the parking lot and his car with a steady sprinkle falling from the sky. He pressed the remote on his key fob, popping the locks on his Lexus. His phone rang. He fished the cell from his belt and glanced at his watch. His mind veered to the flight he needed to catch. With a two-hour drive back to LA, that gave him an hour to pack and an hour to negotiate traffic on the way to the airport. He'd be in Philadelphia, celebrating his first holiday home with his family in eight years, by about midnight local time.

The first sense of excitement Josh had truly experienced in a year pushed into his chest.

He pulled the driver's door open and answered the call. "Marx."

"Hey, buddy. Can't believe I got you on the first try."

Josh didn't immediately recognize the voice, but he did know that rough connection—

"Happy anniversary, dude," the caller said. "How's retired life? Do I have a lot to look forward to?"

"Beck?" Josh asked, picturing his teammate—skull-cut dark hair, nearly black, laser-sharp eyes, slightly crooked nose. "Is that you?"

"It's me," he said, upbeat. "How the hell are you, man?"

"Good, great," Josh lied, his brow tightening as he tried to work out Beck's reason for calling—the happy anniversary bit was complete bullshit. A flash of electric current stung Josh's gut, and his smile dropped. "Are you all right? Are the guys all right?"

"Yeah, fine. Everyone's fine. Didn't mean to worry you."

Josh's body uncoiled, and he slumped into the leather surrounding him as the sprinkles outside turned to fat drops. He closed his eyes, rested his elbow on the window ledge, and pinched the bridge of his nose. "Shit, you know how to give a guy a heart attack."

Beck's rough laugh crossed the line. "You're goin' soft."

"Gone. Long gone." Josh opened his eyes and stared out the rain-blurred windshield toward the ocean.

Hearing from Beck automatically made him think of Grace. In many ways, losing her had left a bigger hole in his life than losing his career. "Where are you?"

"Same place you left us, man. Going out on a sneak-and-peek in about twenty." Which meant the team had been deployed back to Syria. "Gonna get the chance to nail the guy who took out your shoulder."

"No shit." The pain he'd temporarily forgotten about

throbbed back to life. "Give him an extra bullet for me, would you?"

"My pleasure, brother. Hey, could you do me a favor while I'm tracking him down?"

"Anything, anytime."

"Could you get a hold of Grace for me?" he asked. "She's not answering my calls."

Grace.

The image of Beck's ex-wife filled Josh's mind as he'd last seen her, sitting on the edge of his hospital bed, over a year ago now. Her strawberry-honeyed hair had been short and sleek. Her cheeks pink. Blue eyes sparkling with excitement and affection when she'd taken his hand in hers with a shy smile and an

"I've been thinking..."

He pushed the hurt back. "Why? What's going on?"

"I don't know. We were talking pretty regularly up until about three, four months ago, but she seemed distant, you know? Maybe a little evasive. Then she stopped answering my calls, and she's not returning my messages, texts, or e-mails."

"Hold on," Josh cut in. "Beck, she doesn't have to call or text or e-mail you back—you've been divorced *three years*." And, yes, dammit, Josh was counting...not that it made any difference. A hundred years could have passed, and Grace would still be off-limits. "She's probably seeing someone. And if that's true, you're putting her in a really awkward position. Nothing like having your ex call in the middle of the night to cause problems."

"That's not like Grace, but I'd let it go if..." Beck heaved a sigh, and his voice grew serious. "See, it's like this—I'm worried about her. I heard a rumor, and I just need someone I trust to check in on her."

"A rumor? Seriously? Dude, I'm about to leave for Christmas in Philadelphia."

"Can you stop in San Diego on your way? You know I

wouldn't ask you to do this if it wasn't important." His voice lowered as if he feared being overheard. "See, I met a guy from team four on an op out of—" He paused abruptly. "Uh, anyway, we were talking about fishing for marlin in Mexico. I pulled up Facebook and showed him pictures of our trip, that really awesome first anniversary trip Grace and I took—"

Awesome? "The one where you made her go deep-sea fishing with you?" Josh said more than asked.

"Yeah, and—"

"And she puked over the side for eight hours. Dehydrated herself so bad, she landed in a Mexican hospital. That *awesome* anniversary trip?"

"Dude," Beck said in a perfect Dumb and Dumber impression. "Focus."

The man was one of the sharpest SEALs Josh had ever known. A man Josh would always trust at his back. A true brother. But he was also an epically dense husband. Always had been.

"Right," Josh said with an eye roll. "Sorry. Go ahead. Your romantic trip to Mexico..."

"So this guy from four points right at Grace in a picture and says, 'You let your girl strip?' I'm, like, what the fuck, right?"

Denial hit Josh first. Grace Ashby was not the stripping type. She was the sweet girl-next-door type, complete with a smattering of freckles, a smile like sunshine, and the manners of a Southern belle, even though she was a southern California girl, born and bred.

"Come on, Beck," Josh said. "Use your common sense."

"I have been. For two months." Beck's voice came out flat, the matter-of-fact tone he used only when he was serious. "And now I'm worried."

Beck—the warrior—was worried.

Fuuuuuuck.

"This was a SEAL from team four who fingered her with no doubt, dude," Beck said, "not some average Joe."

Josh's denial melted into a blend of shock and confusion. Yes, Grace was a dancer. Her mother, Carolyn, loved to brag and tell stories at the SEAL family get-togethers whenever the team was stateside.

And Carolyn had told the story of Grace starting ballet at three years old, continuing with every type of dance imaginable throughout her life. She'd told stories of Grace smoking the gymnastics team and leading the cheerleading squad all through high school. And Josh knew from his own friendship with Grace that she'd gone on to teach and dance through several different Southern California theatres.

But the transition from dancing to stripping was a huge leap.

He took a moment to force that image up in his mind. But all he could see was that sweet-as-sugar smile and all the sparkling joy in her blue eyes. He couldn't remember ever hearing an inappropriate word come out of her mouth. She was conservative. Politically correct. A pleaser. A nurturer. Being raised by a single mother had given her a fierce independent streak, but Josh believed he knew Grace well enough to know that stripping was way outside her comfort zone.

"The guy was probably drunk off his ass," Josh offered for lack of a better explanation.

"Probably, which is why this will be a snap for you, bro. All I need to know is that you set your eyes on her. If you could just go down there, pop in at the town house, talk to her, *see* her, get the real story, I'll know she's okay. I trust you, man. If you say she's safe, I'll know she's safe. Then I'll be square."

Square.

Every SEAL had to be emotionally, mentally, and physically square before heading out on a mission.

Distraction led to mistakes. Mistakes led to death.

Beck might be square after Josh put eyes on Grace, but Josh would be fucking skewed.

Then again, Josh wasn't going out on a mission.

He sighed. "What club?"

"Thank you so much, man. I knew I could count on you. The guy said he saw her at Allure. It's the same place that used to be Teasers."

The name of the dive bar made Josh wince. They'd both spent years in San Diego, and while Josh didn't frequent the strip clubs, many other navy personnel did, and he'd heard every story.

"It's not the sleazy joint it was a few years ago," Beck continued. "It's been taken over by a new owner and gone high-class. But I googled the place and found out there was a murder in the parking lot just a week ago."

"I'll take care of it." Josh dropped his head back against the seat again, mentally reworking his schedule. If he wasn't going home for Christmas, he could take the opportunity to clean up his town house—one in the same development as Grace and Beck's—now that the renters had moved out. He needed to get that thing up for sale. But he also needed this holiday with his family.

"Thanks, man." Relief rang clear in Beck's voice, even eight thousand miles away. "I owe you."

"No." A flash of memory tightened his throat—Josh lying on a pile of rubble drenched with his own blood in Aleppo, the deadliest city in Syria. Over eighteen months later, and he could still remember the feel of Beck's body weight hitting him as his friend provided cover against enemy fire after the IED had exploded. He released a long exhale. "You'll never owe me."

2

Josh tapped his fingers on the steering wheel to the beat of Nickelback's "Feelin' Way To Damn Good," wishing he could agree. But he was sick. And worried. And anxious .

Swish-swish.

The wipers cleared a path across his rain-spattered windshield, allowing the pink neon advertising Allure, a gentlemen's club, to flash against the black sky, mocking him. He'd never believed he'd get this far. On the drive here, he'd convinced himself that this was all a misunderstanding. That this would turn out to be a case of mistaken identity. That Grace was still doing nothing racier than coaching high school cheer teams and was perfectly fine.

But when he'd reached her town house, he'd discovered Grace didn't live there anymore. And when he'd swung by her forwarding address, he'd found himself in a neighborhood where young men loitered on the corners in small groups.

Swish-swish.

The realization that he was only yards away from Grace inside that club turned him inside out. There were ways he could get out of the duty while accomplishing the end goal, but the truth was, he craved the sight of her again.

He scanned the parking lot, searching for the high-end Jeep SUV Beck had given Grace their last Christmas together. The fact that it wasn't anywhere in the lot meant one of two things— she either wasn't here or she'd sold the car just like she'd sold the town house.

With stress building, Josh turned off the engine and pushed open the car door. The wipers stopped midswish, and the music cut out. He stood, locked the doors, and slipped the keys into the pocket of his blazer. Traffic raced past on the freeway with a soft whoosh, and the club's music thumped through the evening mist. The chill December air swept in, turning his nervous sweat to ice, and Josh shivered as he started toward the club's front door.

The parking lot was filled with high-end sedans, sports cars, and SUVs. Christmas lights lined the club's eaves. He paused at the front doors, painted with sexy female caricatures in skimpy elf costumes, and replayed his cover story while dragging cash from his wallet. He'd only been to strip clubs three times in his life—all three for bachelor parties—but he'd only needed to go once to understand how they operated. He folded the bills and pushed them into his front pocket.

As he gripped the cool metal door handle, his muscles coiled tight, and his mind focused on the mission. But he sure as hell wished he were breaching a dozen terrorists with AK-47s in a Taliban stronghold instead of the lone, pretty, little Grace Ashby at a strip club.

He stepped into a foyer thumping with the sexual beat of My Darkest Days' "Nature of the Beast." Two walls were painted black, two covered in smoke-colored mirrors. A man who could have passed for three guys stuffed into one suit turned toward

Josh. He looked Hawaiian or Samoan with a round face, dark skin, black eyes, and a buzz cut. And he was *huge*. At least three inches taller than Josh's six foot one and tipping the scale at over three fifty.

"Welcome." His voice was deep and flat and serious. "There's no cover charge, but we have a two drink minimum. We ask that you be as generous as possible to the staff, seeing as it's Christmastime and all."

"How 'bout I start with you?" Josh drew cash from his pocket, offering the man a fifty. "I understand a friend of mine works here. Her name is Grace."

The man's dark eyes flicked to the bill, then back to Josh's face, but his body never moved and his hands remained at his sides. "I'm sorry, sir, I can't give out personal information on the girls."

The girls.

Josh's stomach twisted. The sweat gathering on his neck slid down the indention of his spine. He swallowed the ball in his throat and pressed the money into the bouncer's massive hand. "I'm a friend, and I need to tell her something about her family."

The man's fingers curled around the money. "I just saw her out on the floor. But she goes by Nicole here, so don't call her Grace. And don't interfere with her work," he warned, his voice growing hard, "or I'll *hurt* you."

Josh acknowledged the bouncer's threat with a single nod, then took a deep breath, and strolled into the main club. He should feel relieved—he'd found her. But working the floor meant she was soliciting lap dances from spectators. He held on tight to denial while apprehension wound deep in his gut along with a hundred unanswered questions.

He immediately swept the club for layout, exits, and head count. A large, curved stage took up the most real estate, the glass base sleek and dotted with three stripper poles. Beneath the glass, lights faded on and off, making the floor glow in sensuous blues and violets, but the women dancing on the stage needed no enhancements. A blonde swayed on the far left leg of the stage, her major assets: enormous tits. A redhead writhed against the gold pole center stage, generous hips pumping. And a tall, leggy Asian woman rocked the stage on all fours to the right. Each wore nothing but heels or boots and a feathered or sparkling G-string.

Despite his distaste for these clubs, Josh's blood heated and his cock tingled with a surge of lust, reminding him it had been way too long since he'd gotten laid. Like an idiot, he'd been holding out for Rachel. Since she'd jetted to the east coast with that head case, Ryker, Josh had been working too much to get into dating. And the whole one-night-stand thing worked better for him as a SEAL, when he'd only been in town for a few days before heading off on another mission. Now when he took a woman to bed, there was nowhere to hide the next day. Or the next week. Or the next month. And he hadn't met anyone he wanted to promise he'd call in the future.

" Nature of the Beast" transitioned into something slower that Josh didn't recognize, a song with a thick, sensual beat and nasty rap lyrics about pulling hair, a man of steel, and candy rain. The powerful beat throbbed beneath Josh's feet and straight up his legs. On stage, three more women emerged from behind crimson draperies, while those who'd been dancing, pranced out of sight. The whole switcheroo had been both entertaining and smooth, and the new girls, wearing a variety of outfits covering all their assets at this point, moved with slow sashays and gyrating hips.

He pulled his gaze from the new performers and scoped out the bar, which filled one long wall of the club. He needed to get a look at all the women on the floor to eliminate the possibility that the Grace he was looking for worked there.

Two female bartenders worked behind the heavy, shiny wood expanse, wearing red lace corsets and velvet Santa hats. Two more women stood by holding trays, wearing some sort of elf suit. Their emerald-green skirts were trimmed in white faux fur and so short, their black-lace-covered ass cheeks showed.

Their matching halter-style tops were cut deep in the front, exposing plenty of plump cleavage. And their boots—thigh-high, sleek, and black patent, like their low-slung belts.

Josh immediately pictured Grace in that outfit—or at least tried. But his mind couldn't fit those puzzle pieces together. As long as Josh had known her, Grace had never worn anything more revealing than a sundress.

Josh pushed his hands into his pockets and wandered toward the bar, where he leaned against a stool, searching every elf for Grace's cute little strawberry-blonde bob. Booths lined the walls, individual tables took up the center of the club, and premium plush seating ringed the stage up front, where men called out to the women and slipped dollar bills into sparkling G-strings.

Several dancers milled among the patrons, chatting, touching, taking them by the hand and leading them up a spiral staircase to private rooms. Josh had never been in one, but he knew exactly what went on in there—guys were not shy about spilling every detail of their strip club encounters. The thought of Grace selling herself that way made him sick and doubled his determination to get to the bottom of whatever was going on with her.

"Hey, handsome. Haven't seen you here before."

Josh didn't exactly startle at the seductive female voice behind his left shoulder, but his muscles went rigid. He turned to face a tiny woman with big brown eyes—and big, bouncy tits barely covered in a green velvet halter. She too wore a Santa-style hat, this one green to match the elf getup, sporting a big fluffy white fur ball at the point. She caressed the sleeve of Josh's sport jacket with one hand, the other holding an empty tray against her hip.

"I'm Stephie." She tipped her head and looked up at him through thick black lashes heavily coated with mascara. "Why don't you buy me a drink while we get acquainted?"

A heavy, powdery scent wafted off her, along with her body heat. His nerve endings seemed to spread along the surface of his skin and sing to attention. Which meant, yeah, definitely too little sex in way too long, because she wasn't his type at all.

"Actually…" He pulled a twenty from his pocket. "I'd appreciate it if you could point out Nicole for me."

Her eyes lowered to the bill, then returned to his, a sly little smile on her lips. She slipped the twenty from Josh's fingers with an enthusiastic "Easiest twenty I've made all night."

She turned and pointed toward a shadowed corner where a group of rowdy younger men sat near the stage. A woman stood between two chairs, her back facing Josh. She was leaning forward, her hands braced on the men's shoulders.

The woman who went by Nicole wore a one-shouldered, skintight black dress that clung to every luscious curve and barely covered her ass. Tanned legs stretched long and lean beneath the hem, made even longer—and sexier—by the sparkling spiked heels she wore. One side of the dress had diamond-shaped cutouts, showing a nice amount of evenly tanned skin all along her body, right down to her hip.

The fabric gathered and was held together with clear rhinestones down her side. There was no way she was wearing anything underneath.

Josh didn't recognize her as Grace. This woman had copper-colored hair falling in curls to the middle of her back. Right color—wrong length. And Grace had always been thin, with a more boyish straight-up-and-down figure. Josh would have noticed curves like those.

Wouldn't he?

"In the black," Stephie said. "Nicole. That's who you're looking for, right?"

"Don't think that's her," he told Stephie. "But thanks."

"Can I get you a drink?"

"Yes, please. Jack and Coke. Double would be good."

"Be right back."

When he slid his blazer off, his bad shoulder pulled, reminding him of the football incident. He tossed it over the back of the chair, and rolled up his sleeves before sitting, his eyes locked on the woman in black, waiting for a glimpse of her face. But his peripheral vision was picking up the brazenly erotic moves on the stage, and combined with the music, the lyrics, and the atmosphere, Josh's body was definitely responding. His cock had grown thick, and the confinement of his slacks added pressure along his length. His heart was beating too fast, his body was too hot, his throat too tight.

The woman laughed, throwing her head back, and her hair —a shade darker than Grace's, he was sure—fell down her spine like a sensual waterfall. A man came up beside her, and she turned and greeted him, exposing the stylishly and incredibly sexily cut side of her dress. Yep, she definitely had amazing curves.

He tried to remember Grace wearing anything that would have accentuated curves but couldn't. Tried to remember feeling them during the occasional hug—again, nothing.

Yes, he'd purposely been trying *not* to notice, considering she'd married his best buddy and fellow SEAL teammate, but still...

She reached up and hugged the older man. Since this wasn't

Grace, Josh let himself survey all that gorgeous skin, taking in her small waist, full hips and, once again, checking out the length of those sleek thighs. And he was plenty warm by the time he lifted his gaze to the woman's face again.

Familiarity burned along his sternum and across his ribs.

Grace.

" Holy...shit..." He stared, trying to convince himself he was mistaken. Her heavy makeup was messing with his mind—Josh had never seen Grace with more than a trace. But then she slid her hands down the older man's arms, rested her fingers in his, and smiled. And that grin was something Josh would never mistake—right down to the right-sided dimple near her mouth.

It's Grace.

His stomach jumped, skipped...and plummeted. Grace was working in a strip club. Wearing a barely there dress that showcased every asset, makeup that turned her from sweet to seductive, and laying her hands all over strange men.

He pushed to his feet, hands clenched, then rethought and sat back down. He had no rights to her. No say in her life. He'd given all that up when he'd walked away.

But he still cared. And she wouldn't be here, doing this, unless something was wrong. He could still help, despite their past.

She continued talking with the older man. They turned toward the stage, leaning into each other, talking over the music, and the man slipped his arm around her waist, his hand settling low on Grace's hip. The intimacy of the touch made Josh's fingers curl into fists.

Stephie showed up with his drink. Josh didn't even give her time to set it on the table. He took it straight from her hand and tipped it back, taking the whole thing in one swallow.

"Ooooh-kay," Stephie said in a half laugh. "I assume that means you'd like another?"

"Please."

The older man moved his hand up her back and kissed Grace on the temple before wandering off through the club. Grace made her way to a dancer straddling a customer's hips near the stage. With a very friendly stroke of her hand over the man's shoulder, Grace glided around behind the dancer, put her hands on the woman's waist, her chin on her shoulder, and let her body follow the movement.

"What in the fuck...?" Josh murmured, unable to pull his gaze from the erotic sight.

Grace's hands slid lower, gripped the woman's hips, and urged them into a sexier roll. She spoke to the client as she thrust, easing the dancer's hips into a more rhythmic thrust. He nodded, eyes big, mouth open like a drooling puppy, and Grace smiled, a sultry, seductive smile Josh had never seen before. The dancer dropped her head back to Grace's shoulder, raised her arms to wrap them around Grace's neck, and turned her face against the skin of Grace's throat.

Patrons sitting nearby cheered their approval of the girl-on-girl action, and the heat simmering in Josh's body rocketed through his groin and up his chest. He fought to search out the what, the how, the why of this, but his mind floated in distracting titillation.

"Here you go." Stephie set Josh's second drink down.

"Thanks. Keep 'em coming, will you?" he asked.

"Who are you?" Stephie asked. "Her new bodyguard or something?"

Josh's gaze broke from the erotic sight of Grace getting it on with two others and focused on Stephie.

"Why? Does she need one?"

"I personally think we all need one after what happened last week. But, no one's springing for any service, so I guess we're relying on our monkeys in suits."

"Stephie!" Someone called from close by. "Need another drink over here, sweetness."

She glanced at Josh again. "I'll bring you another in a few." Then she darted through the shadows to another table.

When Josh returned his gaze to the lap dance, Grace was gone, the original dancer still going at it with her customer.

He scanned the area and found Grace weaving through the club, greeting men, group by group, stopping to talk for a moment, then moving on. No lap dances. No running to get drinks. Josh couldn't figure out the setup.

Josh downed the next drink in two swallows, but the first was already hitting his bloodstream, making him bolder, braver, and —he knew from experience—far more stupid. It also made him forget all about that nagging pull in his shoulder.

When the song changed and the women on stage transitioned once again, Grace watched closely, then scanned the club like an overseer, her gaze pausing on every girl as they worked the room. And Josh could only compare her behavior to a lion watching over her cubs.

He was trying to figure her out while fighting complex emotions he was sure colored his perspective when her gaze passed over him. Then her eyes jumped back and held on his face with a spark of shocked disbelief. A sizzle broke out across his ribs. No turning back now. She'd seen him. She knew he didn't belong here. She knew this wasn't a coincidence.

But having her intense gaze locked on him made his chest ache.

Fuck, he'd missed her. Missed her friendship, her laughter, her quick mind. He hadn't realized until now, their gazes locked yards apart, just how hollow he still felt without her in his life.

Her brow pulled tight. Emotions flashed in her eyes. And Josh felt a direct connection between them across the space. She started forward, never breaking eye contact. Josh took a slow, deep breath and tried to smooth the edge of raw nerves.

Stephie showed up and set his third drink down with a perky "I'll check back."

Josh had never seen Grace look so absolutely stunning. This was not the girl he'd left last year. She'd always been strong and smart. But this woman was more—more secure, more confident, more in control.

Josh had never imagined finding that so damn hot, but watching her walk toward him with all that self-possession was sexier than a brand-new M4 submachine gun.

She paused two feet away, searching his face as if she still couldn't believe he was real. The alcohol had definitely flooded his veins. He couldn't get words out of his mouth while his head and heart were swimming with monologues he wanted to spill all at once.

"Josh?" She dropped to her knees, right there in front of him, hands on his thighs. Those clear blue eyes he'd known so well for so long searched his. "Are you okay?" Her gaze darted to his shoulder, his arm, back to his face. "Is your shoulder okay?"

He managed a nod.

Her hands tightened on his legs. "Has something happened to Isaac?"

His gaze slid lower, to her chest and the way the dress pulled her breasts up and together. She was luscious. A whole different woman than he'd expected to encounter. One that made him crazy with lust.

She cupped his jaw and lifted his gaze to meet hers. "Josh? Is Isaac okay?"

The sweet gesture pulled at all those buried memories. He covered her hand with his. It was small and warm, just like he remembered. "Beck's fine."

"Oh, thank God." Tension drained from her shoulders and the fear in her face cleared as she sat back on her heels. But only a moment of relief passed before confusion...and a little suspicion...filled her eyes. "Then why are you here?" she asked. "And how did you find me?"

Grace glanced at the two empties sitting on the table beside Josh as he reached for another half-filled lowball glass. He was drinking faster than the waitresses could clear.

"Josh?" she asked, prodding him to answer her earlier questions.

"I'm in town on business," he said, voice rough, gaze staring into his drink—which probably meant he was lying. "I tried calling you, but you didn't answer." Now he looked at her, those beautiful eyes of his filled with barely veiled accusation. "So, I stopped by your town house to say hello and found you don't live there anymore."

Oh...shit...

All her muscles tightened up.

"The new owners," he said, "were nice enough to give me your forwarding address."

Oh...double shit...

Her fingers curled into fists against her thighs.

"And your new neighbor tells me you work nights at this club. I'm dying to know how you managed to pick an apartment in the *only* ghetto in San Diego. But we'll get to that later."

His bossy tone set her on edge, and she brought one foot under her to stand. But Josh wrapped his fingers around her forearm and leaned forward, his face just inches from hers. And God, he smelled good.

Just a touch of spice left over from the day and a whole lotta signature Josh. The scent brought memories swimming back—of long, quiet nights sleeping in his hospital room, of slow, challenging days of physical therapy. Of trust built, friendship forged, laughter shared...

Hearts broken.

"Gracie," he said, his voice softening, his eyes stormy. "*What's going on?*"

She tried not to bristle. Logically, she understood he was worried. Emotionally, his concern felt a lot like judgment.

"Nothing's going on." She pulled from his grasp and stood, struggling to balance on her ridiculously high heels. "I'm just working, that's all."

His eyes narrowed. "That's all? Seriously? That's what you're giving me? *That's all?*"

Grace gritted her teeth to keep from saying something she'd regret, but his attitude stung.

The songs changed, and Grace met his gaze with a serious one of her own. "Look, I have to get back to work. If you're still in town tomorrow, maybe we can have coffee...or something..."

"Coffee? Are you fucking *kidding me*?"

Josh pushed to his feet, and Grace fell back a step. She'd forgotten how tall he was. How imposing.

She'd seen him in his navy whites a couple of times, but never in business casual. His muscled body filled out the button-down and the slacks like they'd been tailor-made for his body, and heat kindled low in her belly.

"Gracie," he implored, "you're talking to someone who

knows you. Someone who knows that if you're *here, doing this,* there's something wrong."

That was all it took, one perfectly placed cynical dig, and the sexual heat transitioned into anger. "You don't know *what* I'm doing. You're assuming." She felt others' attentions slide their way, and she forced her voice down. "There's *nothing* wrong, and you sure as shit don't have any right to pass judgment on my life. I'm perfectly fine. Good-bye, Josh."

She turned, hands fisted, and moved quickly toward the black velvet curtain leading to dressing rooms at the back of the club. Her stomach hurt. Her brain spun. Her heart ached.

"Grace, wait." He called behind her, half demand, half plea.

She cringed at the use of her real name but kept moving. Adrenaline surged, burning along her limbs.

She ducked between the drapes and hurried down the walkway, her heels clicking loud on the concrete.

"Grace, stop." His voice sounded right behind her at the same moment he grabbed her arm and spun her around. He gripped both arms and pushed her back against the wall.

After one long, stunned second, she shoved at his chest. "What the hell is wrong with you? You're the last person I expected to manhandle me. *Let. Go. Now.* "

He instantly released her and stepped back. "I'm sorry. I didn't mean to..." Scraping both hands through his hair, he paced. "I just don't know what to think. I'm *worried* about you, Grace."

"Stop calling me that. I don't want people knowing my real name."

He flung his arms out to the side and let them drop to his thighs. "If that doesn't scream *problem*, nothing does."

She crossed her arms, all the hurt and judgment from the past resurfacing like grease on water. "Why do you insist there has to be a problem when I'm telling you there's not?"

"You're working in a *strip club*, Grace. You're dressed in..." He gestured toward her, then groaned out, "God. This isn't right. This isn't you."

"You haven't seen or spoken to me in a year. A lot has happened in that time. You have no right to decide what's me and what's not."

"I've known you for *seven years*." He was growing edgy, a little frantic. "You couldn't have hidden *this*."

She rolled her eyes at his absurdity. "My ex-husband still doesn't know I got my bachelor's degree while we were *married*. The truth is that we all become the people we need to be to get by, the same way you and Isaac became killers to survive as SEALs. I never held that against either of you, and I damn well deserve the same respect, regardless of what work I choose."

"Whoa, whoa..." He put his hands up, his expression twisted in confusion. "Where in the hell is this coming from?"

"It's coming from you, walking in here and passing judgment." She twirled her finger in the air. "So just turn your sweet ass around and get the hell out."

She turned and started walking again, fisting her hands, clenching her teeth, squeezing her eyes shut to force the new wetness back. Chanting *let him go* in her head when she ached to wrap her arms around him for a bear hug. Just to feel him close again.

"Okay, hold on." His hand wrapped around her arm again, but gently. "Let's back up. I didn't mean to turn this into a fight."

No, no, no. That soft, congenial voice tried to crawl into her heart. She couldn't let that happen, because he'd just reject her again. Walk away again. Leave her alone again. It had taken her months to find solid ground after he'd moved to LA. And she was barely holding on to her crazy life now.

"Look," she said, softening her voice and pressing her hands to his chest. His hard, warm chest. She drew a breath. "There is nothing for you to worry about. I truly love this job. I love the club, my boss, my coworkers. The work is fun, challenging, and rewarding. Even the customers appreciate what I do."

"Yeah," he huffed, disgusted. "I could see that."

She threw her arms out to the side and stepped back. "I don't need a fight tonight."

He looked at the ceiling and rubbed a hand over his face with a troubled exhale. She might have toughened up and found her latent sexuality over the last year, but her heart was still as soft as it had always been, and it was killing her to see him so frustrated.

"Put your pea-sized brain to rest, Josh," she told him. "*I'm not stripping.*"

One golden brow lifted in disbelief, and his gaze skimmed down her body.

"God, you're such an ass." She crossed her arms again. "I *talk* to the men. They tell me what moves and routines they like to see from the dancers. I train the girls to do what the men like, which makes them more money. And when they make more money, I make more money. *I'm. Their. Choreographer.*"

That wasn't the job title her boss had given her, but it was the one she'd built around her position as house mom. So, in addition to managing all the girls' needs backstage, which included being a surrogate mother, a psychologist, a makeup artist, a troubleshooter, and a comedian, Grace also taught them how to dance. How to tease and please. And her work had pushed the club onto the top-ten list of strip clubs in San Diego. It had also helped the dancers pay for medical care and school tuition and quality daycare for their kids.

And if the plan she'd put into motion spun out the way she'd planned, she'd slough off the house mom part of the job and take over her very own lucrative niche as dance instructor and choreographer to the area's top entertainers.

But Josh didn't deserve to know her secrets or her dreams.

He gave her a dubious slant-eyed gaze and planted both hands at his narrow hips. "Your job description doesn't matter, Grace. You're still here, still dressed—Jesus, I can't breathe looking at you in that—and you still have to walk across that parking lot where some guy was gutted last week. Strip clubs breed crime—"

"So do liquor stores and Planned Parenthood pickets and TV violence, for God's sake." She was tempted to tell him to go back to the part where he couldn't breathe, but she was sure the tease would have been wasted. "We don't stop driving because someone dies in a car accident. And I'm not going to give up a good job because some assholes drank too much and got in a fight."

SONGS SWITCHED AGAIN—THE fourth change since she'd set eyes on Josh, which meant she'd been gone from the dressing room too long.

She continued the rest of the way down the hall, but paused before turning the corner and glanced back at him. Hands on hips, shirtsleeves rolled up on his forearms, tension drawing all six feet of his amazing body up tight, he looked every bit the commanding presence he'd always been. Overhead lights made his wheat-colored hair shine like the sun. Her heart felt like it was being cut into tiny little pieces, and she cursed herself for one: falling in love with him in the first place, and two: never falling back out.

Her whole chest ached.

"Go home, Josh. There's nothing here for you."

Gracie finger-waved to Beth, the house mom who'd taken over for her at midnight. "Good night, Sadie.

Remember to tell Rebecca to ice her ankle, please."

"Will do." Beth picked up a brush to fluff Clarissa's hair before the dancer took center stage. "Have Theo walk you out."

"Will do."

Grace made her way through the halls toward the front door, exhaustion and heartache dragging at her.

Seeing Josh again, so unexpectedly, had been tough. But sending him away with all the unease still between them left her feeling hollow and depressed. More than anything she needed a friend in her life now. The casual friendships she'd made with the staff at the club were great for everyday conversation and company, but she wished she had someone deeper in her life. Someone who really *got* her. And the reminder that she'd ruined that with Josh really hurt.

There had been a thousand times over the last year when she'd wished she hadn't asked him to move in with her, that she hadn't suggested there was more than friendship between them. Not because it hadn't been true, but because she'd lost his friendship over voicing the reality.

Passing into the foyer, she searched for Theo, the bouncer manning the door. He was speaking to a patron, then ushered him into the club before he turned to Grace.

"What'd you do to that guy, Nikki?" he asked. "He's a mess."

Grace peered toward the bar, where Josh sat slumped on a stool, arms crossed on the bar, head resting facedown on his forearms. His blazer was draped over the stool beside him. And Dean, her boss and the club's owner, was standing thirty feet away, talking to a customer.

"Je-sus." Her heart twisted. "Why'd you let him stay?"

"Because the girls feel sorry for him. Every time I approached him with the intention of pushing him into a cab, Kelly gave me the death stare." Theo's big shoulders lifted in a shrug as if he couldn't help himself. "And everyone really likes him. Even Dean. They sat around talking for over an hour."

At that moment, Dean stepped away from the bar and started through the club toward the entry. He was dressed in his typical slacks, silky button-down open at the collar, with a blazer over the top. He was in his early sixties, was never sleazy with the girls, paid fair salaries, and was generous with his appreciation of the staff's hard work. Which was why she didn't want to lose him as a boss. If Josh had said something—she couldn't imagine what, but something—that would get her in trouble...or fired...she was going to turn homicidal.

"Hey, hey, Nick," he said as he neared, his grin wide and authentic. "Did you hear the crowd going crazy for your Santa Baby number?"

She relaxed and returned his grin. "I did. The girls were amazing. I'm training a few new ones each day. By Christmas, we should have twenty-five doing it at once."

He reached out and tapped her nose. "*You* are amazing. I was telling your friend Josh there all about how you've turned this club into something really special." He glanced over his shoulder toward Josh and laughed, his belly rocking with the sound. "Think I might have just talked him into a coma."

"Um, yeah...sorry about that..."

"Oh, come on. This happens here on a nightly basis. Nice guy. We were both squids once upon a time," he said, using the navy's alternative to "sailor." "He was really interested in your plans for the studio."

Grace grimaced internally, and she thought the skin beneath her left eye might have twitched, but Dean didn't seem to notice. "Well, I'm glad you two hit it off. I'm going to see if I can get him off the stool now."

"Good luck, honey." Dean squeezed her shoulder and winked. "And great job with the girls. You're my star."

She smiled. "See you tomorrow."

She strolled to Josh's side and paused, greeting the bartenders, Sandra and Kelly. "How much did he drink?"

Sandra straightened bottles underneath the counter and gave Grace a sympathetic grimace. "I cut him off when he'd finished half a fifth."

Grace sucked air through her teeth. That was eight shots. "Shit."

Sandra lifted a shoulder, glancing at Josh. "He's a big guy. Averaged about two shots an hour. He'll be okay."

"He's so sweet, Nikki," Kelly said. "Not to mention smokin' hot. Kept his back to the stage all night.

Kept asking when you'd be off. If you aren't keeping him, would you mind giving him my number? I never meet nice guys like that."

Grace sighed and turned her gaze on Josh. His hair was a tousled mess, one closed eye visible beneath the fringe. The sight of his long golden lashes curved against his cheekbone took Grace back to what had seemed like magical months together. From the moment he'd been flown back to San Diego from Syria, Grace had been by his side.

She fingered back the butter-soft strands of hair that had fallen into his eyes. A soft smile turned her mouth, and tears welled out of nowhere. She sniffed them back, then squeezed his shoulder to wake him.

"Josh, time to go home."

His lashes fluttered, but he remained perfectly still as he gained his bearings. Only then did he sit up slowly. He rubbed his face on a heavy exhale. "How long was I out?"

"Not long," Sandra said.

"Maybe ten minutes." Kelly added with a flirty smile. "You can sleep on my bar anytime."

He licked his lips, pulled cash from his pocket, and laid out two hundred-dollar bills, one for each of the women. "Thanks for keeping me company, ladies."

Both Sandra and Kelly lifted their brows at Grace.

"Okay, big spender, where are you staying? And how are you getting there?" She could easily drive him to his hotel, but she was tired and absolutely didn't want to get into another argument.

"Nowhere." He reached for a small bowl of mints sitting on the bar and popped one into his mouth. "I wasn't planning on staying. Shit, I have to call my mom."

He stood and took a few steps away from the bar, the phone at his ear.

"His *mom*?" Kelly asked in a hush. "God, he's adorable. I just want to take him home."

Take him home. That thought lit off flashes all over Grace's body. "He's not *that* adorable. Josh." She lifted her voice and he turned around. "It's too late to call your mom. Three-hour time difference, remember?"

"But they're expecting me..." He rolled his wrist to look at his watch—the same watch Isaac and their entire team had worn. "Ah, shit. They think they're picking me up at the airport... Hey, yeah, Mom," he said into the phone, "it's me. I'm sorry, I didn't make my flight... No, no, everything's fine. I'm still coming. Yes, I promise. Okay. I'll call you tomorrow. Love you."

He disconnected with a groan and sank onto the stool again, dropping his head. "Fuck me."

Kelly's hand shot up. "Yes!" Grace and Sandy shot Kelly a what-the-hell look, and Kelly gave an impish grin and a little shoulder shrug. "Nikki knows my number if you ever have the urge to offer that up again."

Josh chuckled. Then turned his head, still resting against his arms. His eyes were clear, sky blue, sleepy, and scanned her face intimately, caressing every surface from her forehead to her chin. "There's my girl." His mouth tipped up at the corner. "You look twelve years old again."

She'd scrubbed off all her makeup, changed into shorts, a T-shirt, and flip-flops, and thrown her hair into a ponytail. Yeah, she'd probably taken a decade off her looks. And the affection in Josh's eyes when he saw the Grace beneath all the props swelled her heart against her will.

"You didn't know me when I was twelve," she said.

"But I saw pictures. Remember when your mom brought your photo albums to the team's barbecue?"

He laughed. "God that was sweet."

Sandy's hands worked a towel over a glass, but she was shooting Grace her why-exactly-aren't-you-jumping-this-guy look.

The past washed in and took every ounce of comfort from the moment. Grace answered Sandy's silent question with "Long story."

Customers beckoned, and Sandy and Kelly drifted down the bar again.

"You're even more beautiful than I remember," he murmured.

She sighed, running her fingers through his hair. "And you're even more obnoxious." He grinned, that sleepy, sloppy grin that made her insides ache. "Shit, what am I going to do with you?"

He lifted his head and propped it on his palm, then curled the other hand around hers. "Talk to me, Gracie."

Christ, that voice, deep and smoky. Those eyes, bright and intense. He pried her heart open, and Grace felt the year separating them melting away.

"Josh—"

"You sold your town house; you're living in a dangerous neighborhood. Now you're working here.

What happened to cheer coaching at the high school?"

Just like that, her defenses burned to life. "I'm still coaching. The girls are on winter break. We cut back the training schedule."

His brow creased. "You're working *both* jobs? How long have you been here?"

"Nine months."

"Jesus, Grace, what does your mom think about you working at a strip club?"

She sighed, the weight of everything he wanted to know wearing on her patience. "I'm too tired to get into this now. Come on." She pulled on his hand until he stood. "I'll drop you at a hotel."

When she tried to take her hand from his, he laced their fingers and let her guide him through the club, following like a puppy. God, he was so drunk. Which was completely out of character for the Josh she'd known—always in control, always sharp, always on.

Theo stood ready to open the door for them. "Want me to call him a cab?"

"I'll do it, thanks."

"It's raining out there..." Theo warned.

"I know." Grace had seen the rain splashing on the windows in the dressing room, but she didn't care.

She was burning up from the inside out. She could play hot and sexy with the customers all night without getting worked up, but put Josh Marx within eyesight and she felt like she'd burst into flames.

She stepped out into the night and paused under the awning as the club door closed behind them, muffling the music. She took a cleansing breath of the cold, rain-soaked night air, letting some of the stress leak from her shoulders, but an old, familiar ache had settled in her heart.

She pulled her phone from her purse, tapped into the Internet browser, and started searching for hotels nearby.

"Seems like your shoulder healed just like the doctor said it would," she said absently as a website popped up on her screen.

Josh pulled her around to face him, his gaze deliberate. "Okay, what's going on here, Grace? No one's listening. No one's watching. *Talk to me.*"

She narrowed her eyes. "I think you're the one who should be telling me what this is about. Why are you suddenly so concerned?"

"Your whole life has changed in a year, and not for the better. If you needed something, why didn't you call me? Why didn't you tell Beck?"

All the anger and frustration and hurt she'd buried crept in. "First of all, my life might be different, but it's definitely not worse, and that assumption offends me. Second, why in the hell would I call you for anything after you so completely bailed on our friendship? And third, Isaac was never there for me even when we were married. Why would I think it would be any different now?"

She didn't wait for an answer. She couldn't. She'd been holding everything together for so long on her own, she was ready to break. She'd put Isaac and Josh behind her. She had goals now. A direction of her very own. No mother guiding her to an acceptable place in life, no absent husband placing confining expectations on her. No friend stealing her heart.

She turned and walked into the rain. "My life may not look perfect to you, but it's mine, and it's staying that way. Find your own way to a hotel."

Hold it together. Hold it together.

"We may not be perfect, Grace," he said, coming up alongside her, "but Beck and I would have been here for you if you needed us."

She stopped and turned on him, outraged he'd claim such bullshit. "Really? Where is Beck right now?

Oh, wait, classified, right? Let's narrow it down—is he in the United States?" When Josh glanced away, she said, "I thought not. And what about you? When's the last time I heard from you?"

His jaw shifted sideways, gaze lowered to the ground for only a second before he met her eyes with familiar determination. "I'm here now."

Way too little, way too late.

"Ironically, I don't need you now. And I never needed Isaac." She turned toward her car again, and the rain came down harder. By the time she reached the cheap little sedan, her clothes clung to her body.

"Is that why you're not answering his calls?" Josh called behind her. "Because you're too damn stubborn to accept help?"

Grace's feet stopped dead in a puddle. She swung around on her heel and took three steps back toward him before she stopped herself. "*That's* why you're here—Isaac called you." She threw her hands out, caught between fury and heartbreak. "*Of course* that's why you're here—for Isaac. Not for me." She started for the car again, shaking now, but not from the cold or the wet. She was shaking with anger, disillusionment, hurt. So much hurt. "God, I'm so fucking stupid."

Water splashed around her flip-flops and squished through her toes. She should have been freezing, but she only felt numb. Why did she keep falling for physically and emotionally unreachable men? Men who were never satisfied with who she was?

She fumbled with her keys, struggling to find the one for her car through the rain and welling tears.

"He heard a rumor that you were stripping, and—"

Grace pivoted toward him, eyes narrowed. "A *rumor*?" That

was a strange turn of phrase...or maybe she was just oversensitive. "How did he hear a rumor like that when he's all the way across the fucking world?"

"Someone from another SEAL team was here. He recognized you in a photo from your anniversary trip to Mexico."

She closed her eyes. "The trip from hell?"

"Couldn't have been all bad. Beck still has fond memories of—"

"Isaac is clueless, Josh. He may be a good man and an amazing soldier, but he's clueless in just about every other area of his life." She turned away again, muttering, "I'm starting to wonder if that's a prerequisite to become a SEAL."

"Wait, Grace, we can talk this out."

"I don't have anything else to say." Christ, that had come out in her borderline hysterical voice. But she couldn't control the wild emotions as she faced him again. "You already know I'm not stripping. And even if I was, it wouldn't give either of you the right to shove your two cents at me. And, as you can see, I'm perfectly fine. So when you talk to Isaac again, you can tell him I don't need either one of you. Which works out fine, because neither of you ever really wanted me either."

Tears swam in her eyes. Angry tears. Hurt tears. Sick-to-death-of-this-shit tears. She jammed her key into the door lock and clicked it open. Josh pulled her around to face him again, trapping her against the car, and stared down into her face with frustration darkening his expression.

"I didn't walk away because I didn't want you, Gracie," he said, his words so low they were almost drowned by the night sounds. Rain dripped off his straight nose and clumped his golden eyelashes. His smoky blue eyes lowered to her mouth in a languid way that told Grace the alcohol was still singing in his bloodstream. "I walked away because I *did*."

Grace's lips parted with another protective, dismissive

remark, but nothing came out. Her throat tightened into a ball. Her mind teetered between believing the sincere declaration in the moment and brushing it aside.

"Sure. That's why you moved to LA when I told you how I felt." She drew a breath, forcing herself to put self-preservation first. "Here's what I learned during those four long years married to Isaac— *action*, not *words*, is what separates the boys from the men. And I've had more than enough little boys in my life."

His eyes narrowed, and the skin over his cheeks tightened. His lips thinned. And God, he was beautiful, his bronze skin contrasting with his crystal-blue eyes.

"I'm not Beck," he rasped. "And I'm no kid either."

"Kids run when they're scared. Which is exactly what you—"

His hands tightened on her arms. His body pressed her against the car. The surprise of cold steel at her back and warm muscle at her front made her gasp and close her fists in the wet folds of his shirt. He lowered his head, pressing his body into hers. A rigid erection indented her lower belly and burned hot beneath his zipper, stealing Grace's breath. Her body flooded with surprise, confusion...and lust.

"Damn right you scare me," he murmured, his lips an inch from hers. "You're the only thing that's ever scared me, Grace."

Her mind didn't have time to process what that meant, because Josh's mouth sealed over hers, cool and wet and firm. The deliberate press of his lips stunned her for long seconds, while thoughts snapped in her brain like firing synapses. She'd never believed he'd ever cross that line. There had been so many times in the past, perfect moments for their first kiss, but he'd always backed off.

Now, he groaned, the sound a combination of pleasure and frustration. He tilted his head, curved one hand around the back of her neck, and this time when he kissed her again, he meant it

—lips parted, searching, suckling. His other hand slipped around her waist and dragged her up against his body.

Her brain scrambled. Let go and enjoy, or push back to safety? Swoon or rail?

She shouldn't give in to temptation. She knew this was the alcohol taking over. Knew he'd regret kissing her the moment the lust ebbed and his buzz cleared. But then his tongue licked across her bottom lip, her muscles went limp, and her mouth opened. The first sweep of his tongue across hers made her breath catch, made heat rush between her legs. He was hungry, demanding, and far more passionate than she'd ever imagined. The man who'd gone out of his way to deliver appropriate responses, keep respectable distances, and spare her every courtesy, was now fucking her mouth with long strokes of his tongue, exploring in decadent caresses, driving the kiss with hungry urgency.

Grace's mind spiraled. She couldn't think. Couldn't reason. Couldn't make any decisions. She just held on tight, experiencing this lightning strike. Every inch of her skin burned with desire. Every cell vibrated with the thrill of being so desperately wanted by a man she'd craved for years. And she needed more of him. So much more. But somewhere in the back of her mind, she didn't dare ask or even suggest, sure he'd pull away. Again.

She just kissed him back, tasting the hint of whiskey, of mint. The heat, the passion. Letting herself go, letting herself feel his arms around her, soaking in the sounds of pleasure in his throat. She opened her mind to take in every rock of his hips, every squeeze of his hand, every breath lifting his chest, so she could save them in her memory banks for the future.

His mouth slid off hers, kissing a trail across her cheek, resting his forehead against her temple. "God, Grace..."

His hands slid down her sides, curved over her waist, cupped her hips. Grace shivered—a combination of his words, his touch, and the cold. She wanted to tell him how good he felt, how much she wanted him, but feared if she spoke, she'd break this fragile bubble in time. Instead, she wrapped her arms around his shoulders and scraped her fingers through his wet hair. How many times had she dreamed of doing this? Hundreds? Thousands?

God, he felt good. Big. Strong. Hard. Hot. Wet.

It had been so long since she'd been wanted like this. She pulled on his shoulders and lifted herself up his body, the same way she pulled herself up the stripper pole. He gripped her waist, settling her open thighs around his hips and her ass on the car's trunk, pressing his rigid cock to her heat with a long groan into her mouth.

She rocked her hips into him, sliding her sex along his length. He broke the kiss on a long "Oh, Gracie..."

She pressed her face to his neck and bit her lip against her need to say his name. Her need to tell him she needed him inside her—right here, right now, in the parking lot, in the rain.

He pressed her against the car and rocked his hips into her, simulating a long, deep thrust. She couldn't keep the high-pitched cry of pleasure from escaping her throat. Then his hands moved beneath her tee, pushing the wet fabric over her breasts. She hadn't bothered with a bra, and now he bent his head, watching as he took her gooseflesh-textured breasts into those big, strong, scarred hands and stroked roughly, brushing her nipples with his thumbs.

Sensation flooded her chest and arched her back on a soft "Yes."

"So fucking beautiful." His head lowered, and the warmth of his mouth covered one breast.

His name echoed in her head, lay heavy on her tongue, but she held it back, wanting more. Needing more. He sucked her nipple against the roof of his mouth with a growl of lust that vibrated along her skin, and she couldn't hold back the sound that rolled out of her.

Pleasure washed her body, her mind, her soul. She groaned and arched. Rain tapped her face. Cold and hot spiraled through her body. So alive. So free.

"More," she moaned, fisting his hair, lifting her hips against his. His mouth released one breast only to move to the other, freeing another bubble of delicious sensation at the center of her body. "Fuck...

Josh..."

He paused. Exhaled heavily. Then pulled back, sucking her nipple from his mouth and making her shiver. He dropped his forehead to her chest. His quick breaths bathed her skin with heat. Her body ached and throbbed. She needed more. Needed *him*.

"Come home with me," she whispered, combing her hands through his hair. "My place is close."

He rocked his head side to side, then tapped his forehead against her shoulder as if banging it against a wall, his hands fisted in the back of her shirt. "Fuck, fuck, *fuck.*"

His body had gone rigid, his muscles coiled, and an uneasy energy buzzed around him. A flash of panic burned a hole through her chest. This was a huge, *huge* step they should have taken a year ago. She wasn't just going to let him run again.

She used his shoulders to drag herself upright and pressed her mouth to his neck. The hands in her shirt slid down her skin as he pulled the drenched fabric back into place. Even though her instincts told her to keep her barriers up, her heart opened. Hope swelled through her chest, but experience pushed tears to her eyes.

"Look," she said, working for a teasing lightness. "We're still alive. No lightning strike."

His hands rested at her hips, his head on her shoulder, as if he were as much frozen in fear of moving forward as Grace was of him pulling away.

She eased kisses toward his ear, then along his jaw as she slid her hands down his chest, his abdomen, then lower, stroking his erection. His hips rocked into her touch and he groaned. With her free hand, she cupped his jaw and pulled his mouth to hers. She kissed him, licked into his mouth, then whispered,

"Come home with me."

With another groan, he pulled from the kiss with a shake of his head. "Can't." He pressed a hand to his face, rubbed his eyes. "Can't, can't, can't."

She wasn't sure if he was talking to her or trying to convince himself, but he was definitely pulling away.

Hurt flared, drawing anger. She stomped it down, drew on patience, and tried to drag his face up to meet her eyes. But when he lifted his head, his eyes were squeezed shut, as if he couldn't bear to look at her.

"Josh—"

"No," he murmured. Then his eyes opened, and the look there told Grace she'd already lost him. He was miles away. "No, Grace... God... I shouldn't have..."

"We're good together," she insisted, her patience thinning. "We want each other. There's nothing wrong with that."

He stepped back, easing his wet body away from hers with a sucking sound.

"Goddammit." She gripped his forearms and dug her fingers in. "I haven't been Isaac's wife for *three years*. You haven't been his teammate for *a year and a half*. How much time has to pass before it's okay?"

"I...don't know." His expression had gone flat and resolute. "I...just... I don't know."

He pushed away, leaned down, and picked up his soaked blazer from the ground. Grace hadn't even remembered it falling. She wiggled off the fender and gripped his arm. Hurt and anger battled in her chest.

"Josh—"

"I know you don't understand." His gaze drifted down her body, and the pain in his eyes stabbed her heart. He shook his head. "I'm sorry."

He turned toward the club, pulling his phone from his pocket.

She fisted her hands. "Don't walk away from me again, Josh."

He paused, hand on the door, head hanging.

Please turn around.

Please.

But he pulled the door open and disappeared inside.

4
_____

J osh balanced his cell between his sore shoulder and his ear
and jotted down Carolyn Ashby's address. "Twenty-eighth
Street? Isn't that on the east side of Balboa Park?"

"You got it." Pete was an information broker of sorts. Josh
used him for background checks on employees involved in any
consulting job. "And I must say, a much nicer neighborhood
than where her daughter resides."

"Yes," Josh muttered. "Yes, it is." And he was damn well
getting to the bottom of this. Grace didn't have to like it.

Josh glanced down the street from Grace's apartment building, where he'd been waiting for almost an hour. He hadn't been
exaggerating when he'd said the neighborhood was ghetto.
Every building needed work, junk cluttered yards, landscaping
nonexistent or overgrown. Not one house was decorated for
Christmas, and only a few apartment windows had been lined
with lights.

At the corner, not a quarter mile from Grace's car, three
young men loitered. Josh was damn sure he'd seen half a dozen
drug deals go down in the short time he'd been watching.

"How long has her mom been there?" He'd gone to the home

where Carolyn had lived just last year, but, like her daughter, Carolyn had moved on. This time, the current residents didn't have information on a forwarding address.

"Looks like..." Computer keys tapped in the background. "About nine months."

The same amount of time Grace had worked at the club.

"Thanks, man. Talk later."

He disconnected, dropped his head back against the seat as his stomach made another hard roll. He felt like a steaming pile of shit. And not just from the wicked hangover throbbing behind his eyes either. Or the way the rancid 7-Eleven coffee stewed in his gut like acid. No, it was his stupid-ass, bone-deep loyalty that was seriously fucking with him again.

He popped two more Advil, grimacing as he swallowed it down with the brown muck in his coffee cup. Checking the dash clock, he picked up his phone and called his mother.

"Ready to talk about it?" she answered.

"Good morning to you too."

"So, why'd you miss your flight?"

He winced, wishing he could flop into the backseat, curl up,...and die. "Doing a favor for a buddy."

"Mmmm?" she coaxed, her way of telling him she expected more information than that.

"Do you remember my teammate Isaac Beck?"

"Of course. I still send packages to your whole motley crew."

Of course she did. Just like Carolyn Ashby did. Just like Grace used to—before the divorce.

God, even two cups of this mud couldn't wipe her taste from his mouth. The sultry, lust-filled flavor of her tongue still haunted him.

"Well, he needed a favor. And it's taking longer than I expected. I'm not sure what day I'll come in, but don't worry about it. I'll catch a cab home."

She snorted a laugh. "Your father won't have that, and you know it. What's wrong, son? What's this favor Isaac needs?"

He winced. She always knew, dammit. "Nothing big. I'm just helping Grace out. It won't take long."

"Are they back together?" she asked. "I thought they got divorced."

"They did get divorced. It's complicated." So fucking complicated it made him want to smash his head against a wall.

"Hmm." Another one of her all-knowing hums. "Well, just so you know, Grace is always welcome here for Christmas. Carolyn too. Your father has more frequent-flier miles than we'll ever use."

The innuendo in her voice only turned the knife in his chest. His mother had been nudging Josh toward Grace since they'd met at one of the team's first homecomings, when his parents had flown out to the west coast to visit. That had ended, of course, once Beck and Grace were married, but started up again when they'd come to see him in the hospital and found Grace asleep in the chair beside his bed. "Jesus, Mom, don't start."

"I'm starting nothing," she said in her crisp, matter-of-fact tone. "There was something between you two years ago. You always did make things more complicated than they had to be." A quick sigh transitioned into "I've got to go. Your favorite peach pies are cooking, and I don't want to hear you bitch about burnt crust. Love you, son."

A reluctant smile turned his mouth. "Love you too."

Josh disconnected, and the second he looked back up toward Grace's apartment, she came down the stairs. She was dressed in shin-length workout pants and a sporty tank top, her long hair wound into a messy knot on the back of her head. And, shit, that outfit framed every luscious curve and toned muscle in her tight little body.

In flip-flops again despite the cold, rainy December day, she jumped a puddle with angelic grace and half jogged, half skipped to her car. His heart lifted, squeezed, and ached, all at the same time. She was the most adorable little thing on the face of the fucking planet. So much stronger, smarter, and more savvy than he'd given her credit for. And way sexier. *Way*.

He could have had her last night. Had that strong, slim body wound up in his. Could have felt every part of her. Touched and tasted his fill. Driven deep inside her. Been surrounded by her. Could have heard her whisper, moan, scream his name. *His* name.

She could have been his. Even if just for the night. Hell, just for the moment.

After feeling her in his arms, experiencing the passion she kept bottled up, he knew making love to her would blow his fucking mind. He craved the luxury of giving himself over to the desire, a desire that would turn into an all-consuming passion if he really let himself go.

The only thing he'd ever wanted as much as he wanted Grace now, was to become a SEAL.

And at the moment, he had neither.

Grace slipped into her piece-of-shit '90s-something Honda and cranked the engine three times before it started.

He swore under his breath. She shouldn't even be living in this neighborhood, let alone driving a car that could break down on her. She pulled away from the curb, and Josh let her get two blocks ahead before he followed.

His cell rang with a blocked number, and he answered through his car's automated system. "Marx."

"Did you find her?" Beck asked over a crackling connection.

Josh's mind flashed with the memory of pushing her wet shirt up, skimming his hands up her tight, warm belly, taking her plump, soft breasts in his hands, and covering one rosy-tipped mound with his mouth. His eyes closed on an involuntary moan, and he cleared his throat to cover. His desire turned him inside out with lust...and clenched his stomach with guilt.

"Yes, I found her," he said. "And she's fine."

"What's going on with her? Why isn't she calling me back?"

She'd never given him an answer about that. "She's working," he ad-libbed. "It's Christmas. She's just busy, dude. We didn't get much time to talk. But you don't have to worry about her. I'm checking everything out, making sure she's square."

"Oh, great," Beck exhaled in relief. "I know you haven't had much time. It's just that we're headed out again, and I don't know when I'll be able to call. The targets weren't where they were supposed to be.

Lousy fucking CIA intelligence."

Josh pictured the team wandering around in the background, collecting equipment, checking gear.

Knew there would be an intense silence over the camp as they all focused on the mission. A sustained adrenaline level almost tangible in the air. Hell, he missed that. And a hot streak of envy only added to the mess in Josh's chest.

He followed Grace through town at a safe distance. She was headed toward Balboa Park, away from the high school where she taught the cheerleading squad, away from the club.

"What about the strip club?" Beck asked.

Fuck. Josh stopped at a red light with Grace four cars in front of him and squeezed his eyes shut. He just couldn't break this kind of news to Beck over the phone. Besides, Josh was realizing it wasn't any of Beck's damn business—any more than it was Josh's. But...shit. This nagging sense of loyalty felt like a goddamned trick monkey on his back.

"She's not stripping," he said. "I don't know what that guy thought he saw. I'm telling you he had to be plastered off his ass, or maybe he was just trying to rile you—"

"Thank God. I didn't know what I was going to do if she was working at a strip joint."

"I hate to keep pointing this out to you, buddy," Josh said, growing annoyed. "But it's not your call anymore."

"So, is she seeing anyone?"

"Are you listening to me?" Josh lifted both hands off the steering wheel in a what-the-fuck gesture.

This was that dense part of Beck that made Josh crazy. "What the hell difference does that make?"

"Relax. I'm just asking."

The line of cars started moving again, but an odd and deepening nagging sensation played at the base of his neck. Josh suddenly realized he didn't know if she was seeing anyone. He'd assumed she wasn't because of what happened between them, but... The possibility that she had a guy in the wings was an uncomfortable thought.

"I don't know," he said truthfully, more to himself than to Beck. "I don't think so."

"How does she look?" Beck asked.

Josh's temper flared again. "What the fuck? What's going on with you? How could that possibly matter?"

"Are you PMSing?" Beck laughed. "I just haven't seen her in forever, and she stopped sending me pictures—"

"That's because you're *divorced*, dude. D-I-V-O-R-C-E-D, divorced."

"Listen, we're lifting off. I gotta go." His tone was lighthearted. He was blowing off everything Josh had said with his signature this-will-work-itself-out attitude. That might have lowered stress in the field, but Josh was getting a glimpse of how fucking annoying it must have been for Grace to deal with here at home. "I'll check in when I can. Later, dude. And thank you."

Beck disconnected, and Josh sat there with his buddy's thank-you weighing on his conscience. Beck wouldn't be thanking him if he'd known what Josh had let himself do last night, let alone what he'd *wanted* to do...

Grace made another turn, and while Josh had been playing guilt games with his brain, she'd led him straight to Twenty-eighth Street. He dropped back so she wouldn't spot his car in the quiet residential neighborhood, one that was 180 degrees from the one she'd just left. Here, every house was decorated with lights and lawn ornaments. Every home had a Christmas tree filling the front window. When she pulled into the driveway of a large home, Josh parked along the curb of a cross street. She hopped out of her car, jogged the steps, and opened a tall gate in the wrought iron, no-climb fence surrounding the property.

Lights had been wound around the top of the fence, and every inch of the home had some touch of Christmas added— lights along the eaves and roofline, garlands along the porch banister, wreaths on every door, including the garage.

But that fence struck Josh as odd. Every other home on the street was just as well manicured, just as large, but not one had a security fence. He stood from his car and strolled closer. Most Craftsmans were called bungalows for a reason. But this one wasn't small, quaint, or cozy. The house rambled, filling a huge lot with pristine tan siding, charcoal gray roof, and a shiny hunter-green front door.

He angled to read a large sign posted on the fence.

Safe Haven Guest Home.

An uncomfortable pressure built in his chest. He stopped, stuffed his hands in the pockets of his jeans, rolling the name around in his head several times. "What the hell...?"

Pulling out his phone, he googled the name along with San Diego, tapped the page that came up first, and knew he had the right website by the image of the home on the main page. The short description read: *A loving, secure, assisted-living program focused on memory care. Lovely private rooms, structured activities, and experienced staff.*

"Memory care." He shook his head, still confused, then dialed Pete back. "What the hell is memory care?"

"Sup boss?" Pete answered.

"That address for Carolyn Ashby," he said. "Was that her work address?"

"I don't think so. Hold on a sec..." Rustling papers sounded over the line, more keys clicking, and every passing moment developed a whole new layer of sickening dread in Josh's gut. "No. That is her home address. She has no work address."

Josh rested his forehead in his hand. Fuck. Everything Grace was doing suddenly made sense. Perfect sense.

"Oh my God." He rubbed his hand down his face. He couldn't have fucked up any worse. "Shit, Pete, can you do me a quick favor? That address is for a private home care facility for something called memory care—"

"That's a nice way of saying Alzheimer's or dementia. My grandmother went to a home like that."

Josh's shoulders sagged. His brow furrowed. Nine months. Grace had been suffering and struggling with this for nine months? Alone?

"Can you find out how much the facility costs?"

"Looking. But I can tell you it's expensive," Pete said, fingers tap-tap-tapping. "And insurance doesn't cover it. I remember because my mom was my grandma's only living relative, and the cost nearly bankrupted our family."

"Just..." Josh rubbed his eyes. "Text it to me, would you?"

"Done. Later."

Pete disconnected, but Josh stood there a long time, letting everything gel in his mind. There were still questions, but the big ones had pretty much just been answered—Grace was working at the club to pay for her mother's care.

His chest felt both hollow and full. Tears wet his eyes.

If he hadn't already been in love with Grace, he'd have fallen hard that very second.

He took a minute to get his emotions together before heading inside. He hadn't anticipated seeing Grace again after his royal fuck-up last night, knowing she wouldn't want anything to do with him. But that wasn't an option anymore. She needed a friend. And, like it or not, she was stuck with him.

He entered through the tall gate, which made more sense now, and approached the double front doors.

He cleared his throat, planted his hands at his hips, and stared at his shoes. While his thoughts darted in five different directions—Beck, Carolyn, Grace, the club, his own scheduled vacation—his heart filled with purpose.

His cell buzzed, and he pulled it from his pocket to find Pete's message.

Safe Haven runs $6300 a month for full care of Alzheimer's patients. Ashby has no personal long-term insurance, but she does have Medicaid, which covers very little. Ashby's doctor visits and medication are partially covered by Medicare. Family picks up the bulk of the overall cost for care.

Which meant Grace was footing a monthly bill of some-where between four and five thousand dollars.

He sucked a deep breath, blew it out, and knocked.

A muffled female voice called, "Come on in."

With a hive of bees buzzing in his chest, Josh pushed the door open and glanced into the foyer.

"I'm in the kitchen," the woman said from somewhere deeper in the house.

He stepped into the small tiled foyer and shut the door. The thick, fresh scent of pine hit him first, which he guessed was coming from the tree in the window of another room facing the street. This formal living room had been decorated elaborately with pine branches and holly leaves on the fireplace mantel, and prettily wrapped presents stacked alongside the brick hearth.

Two elderly women—much older than Grace's mother—sat on either end of a blue sofa watching television. Neither took their eyes off the set when Josh walked in. Both sat upright and still, hands in their laps, reminding Josh of a pew in church. The rosary sliding through one of the women's fingers might have helped that impression along.

"Hi there." Josh stepped into the living room, and both women turned to look at him.

The woman with the rosary returned her attention to the television without a word. The other woman did the same but pointed at the screen with a pride-filled "That's my husband, right there, Regis."

Josh glanced at the TV where Regis Philbin, a popular morning talk-show host from years past, was interviewing a celebrity in what had to be a rerun. Josh's rough age calculation made the statement possible but, he guessed, highly implausible.

"Really," he said, sliding his hands into the front pockets of his jeans. "He's a pretty big celebrity."

The woman nodded, her smile blissful. On screen, applause erupted, and Josh glanced over to find Philbin speaking to the camera with a grin, a wink, and a "We'll be right back. Don't go away."

"That was just for me," the supposed wife said, never taking her gaze off the television as a commercial for toothpaste replaced the talk-show rerun. "That smile, that wink. Just for me. And the message too." She sighed dramatically. "He's such a sweet man." She seemed lost in her own world a long moment before she popped out with "Tammy's making tuna sandwiches for lunch."

Josh was still trying to find the relevance in the two

disjointed topics when movement drew his gaze to the room beyond. A woman in her early sixties with black-and-silver hair, wearing a bright red, *kiss-the-cook* apron , appeared in an archway, wiping her hands on a kitchen towel.

"Oh, hello. I'm sorry. I thought you were one of our regulars." She started through the living room and offered her hand. "I'm Tammy, owner of Safe Haven."

"Josh—" he started.

"Tammy," the older woman interrupted. "Did you just see Regis wink at me? He knows I love it when he does that."

"Handsome devil," Tammy responded. Then to Josh, "Do you mind talking in the kitchen? I'm making lunches."

"Sure." He followed her past a dining table that could seat twelve and into a large kitchen where the wall over the sink was lined with windows looking out onto a garden. At the center of the garden, Grace sat at a table with Carolyn.

At first glance, Josh's heart took a hit. Carolyn, the vibrant, funny, free-spirited sixty-five-year-old, had aged ten years since he'd last seen her. On the table, a bowl of cereal...Cheerios...sat between the women who were each threading them onto a piece of yellow yarn.

"How can I help you?" Tammy asked.

Josh refocused on Tammy. She leaned her hip against the counter, where bread was laid out next to a large bowl of what clearly looked and smelled like tuna salad. "Sorry to interrupt. I'm a friend of Grace and Carolyn. I don't know how your visitor rules work... I'm just in town for a few days and thought I'd stop by..."

"Josh..." Tammy said thoughtfully, shifting toward the counter and scooping a spoonful of salad onto one piece of bread. "Oh , *Josh*." She turned again, face open with excitement. Her eyes were light and bright, some shade of hazel. "Navy SEAL?"

He smiled, confused, but comfortable with this warm welcome. "Former, yes."

"Right, right. A shoulder injury?"

His confusion deepened, unsure who'd been talking about him, Carolyn or Grace.

"Oh, I've heard so much about you." Tammy gestured with the spoon, and a dollop of tuna salad hit the tile. "Oh dear... I'm sorry."

Josh grabbed a paper towel from the roll on the sink. "No worries. I've got it."

"Thank you. I'm so excited to finally meet you. Carolyn talks about you nonstop when she's lucid. My, oh my, she couldn't have been more proud of you if you'd been her own son."

"I think you have me mixed up with her former son-in-law, Isaac Beck. He's also a SEAL."

"No, no, I know all about Isaac. And all the other men in your team. I think there was a Boomer, Digger, Big Joe... But there's no doubt you were her favorite. Yep, I've heard all about you, Mr. Charmer." Her grin made Josh wonder just what Carolyn had said. "Carolyn will be so thrilled you're here— Oh..."

She trailed off as if she'd just remembered something, and a shadow darkened her expression.

"What?" he asked when she didn't continue.

"It's just... She's having a rough day, and there's no guarantee she'll remember you. People from the past can be a positive trigger, bringing back a whole range of memory, but they can also cause stress and anxiety, which...well...

"I'm sure Grace has told you that Carolyn hasn't recognized her since Betty passed. That was her roommate." She shook her head and gazed out the window at the women. "It's been really rough on Grace.

I'm so glad she has someone to lean on now. We all need

that, don't we?" She smiled sadly at Josh. "Even you big strong SEALs lean on each other, right?"

"I've got you covered, buddy. They'll have to get through me to get to you." Beck's words to Josh on that horrible day filled his head.

Josh cleared his throat, emotions cluttering his heart. "Yes, ma'am. Everyone needs help once in a while." He watched Grace and Carolyn through the window. "I was surprised to hear about this. Carolyn is so young..."

"She's about ten years younger than average for memory issues, but not the youngest resident I've had here. Last year, we lost a fifty-eight-year-old woman who'd been suffering for somewhere between five and seven years."

Josh's heart sank, and he nodded in acknowledgment of Tammy's statement.

Outside, an angry outburst drew Josh's gaze back to the women. With a frustrated cry, Carolyn slapped her hands on the table. She hit the bowl, shooting Cheerios everywhere. And when the little Os hit her, she screamed, batting them away like bees. Josh gripped the counter with one hand, muscles coiled to act.

"Should we—"

"Not yet." Tammy closed a hand around Josh's forearm. "I'm going to have to stop letting Carolyn do this project." A wry warmth filled her voice. "We string the Cheerios for the birds because she loves watching them through the window, but when she's lucid, she says they look like feathered bowling balls and claims we're promoting sparrow obesity."

Grace jumped up, wrapping her arms around Carolyn from behind, trapping her arms at her sides while she spoke in her ear.

"Grace is really good with her." Tammy's hand eased off Josh's arm, and she set the spoon down. "The less chaos for Carolyn when she has a moment, the better."

Carolyn burst into tears and slumped in her chair. Grace pressed her face to her mother's hair. Then she laid her cheek against her mother's head, rocking her gently, while tears glistened on Grace's cheeks.

"Oh dear..."

The empathy in Tammy's voice resonated in Josh's chest. His eyes burned. His heart ached. And his whole view of his role in Grace's life shifted.

"I can see this isn't the best day for a visit," he said.

"I'm so sorry." Tammy turned an uncertain smile on Josh. "Please come back another time. When Carolyn is in a better place, I know she'll enjoy your visit. I know seeing you with Grace will bring her absolute joy and peace."

Joy and peace.

The thought of staying with Grace, of being her support, brought Josh the same sense of joy and peace...among other emotions.

Yes. He'd definitely be back.

Grace stepped out onto Safe Haven's front porch, feeling hollow, fragile, and bruised all at the same time. The memory of her mother coming unglued because she hadn't been able to thread a goddamned Cheerio onto a freaking piece of yarn burst behind her eyelids again, and her knees buckled. She slid along the door until her butt hit the cement, covered her head with her arms, and burst into tears.

They didn't last long. Maybe twenty seconds. Crying took energy, and after a sleepless night, she was physically drained and emotionally wiped out. The episode with her mother—mild in the scheme of things—had just pushed her over the edge.

Now, she had to go spend three hours at cheer practice

pretending to be bubbly and enthusiastic for twenty-two seventeen-year-olds, followed by another eight hours of teaching women how to be enthusiastically sexy for men looking for a fantasy escape.

Days like this made her want to just give up. The only thing that kept dragging her back to her feet was the thought of how often her mother must have felt just like Grace did now while she'd been raising her alone, working two jobs. And she'd always been there to greet Grace with a smile, dry her tears with soft words of hope, and cheer Grace through life while struggling through her own.

She pushed to her feet and dried her face. She'd be okay. Her mom would be okay. Grace just needed to keep putting one foot in front of the other. Focus kept her moving forward, right up until she found Josh sitting on her hood, cross trainers propped on her bumper, elbows on knees.

Her stomach dropped. Her shoulders followed. But her heart was already shattered and numb. "I can't do this, Josh. I really can't."

He pushed from the hood, his stance relaxed but his expression serious. "When did this happen?"

"Last year. Listen, I have to get to cheer practice—"

"When she came to see me in the hospital, she was perfectly fine."

Grace sighed heavily. "No, she wasn't. She hasn't been fine for nearly five years, she's just been hiding it because she didn't want to burden me." The thought of her mother being a burden after all she'd done for Grace was ludicrous and just pushed her anger higher and her sadness deeper. "She started taking medication two years ago, but it hasn't helped. She was doing better before her roommate died…"

Emotion welled up in Grace's throat, and she couldn't go on.

"Will it get better?" he asked, his voice filled with the same distress Grace had lived with for the past year.

"No." The word came out half rasp, half whisper. The will to keep all her emotions stuffed away made Grace tremble.

Josh approached her in slow, thoughtful steps. She wanted to back away, but the utter emotional defeat had robbed her of the will to move. And when he wrapped her in his arms, she squeezed her eyes closed, buried her face in his T-shirt...and broke. Just started bawling.

His arms tightened as he pressed kisses to her hair. Stroked her back. Rocked her gently from side to side. Her second jag in ten minutes dried up as quickly as the first.

"I want to help," he murmured in that low rumbling voice.

Again, too little, too late.

She knew she should let go and step back, but, God, she needed someone to lean on so badly. "There's nothing you can do. There's nothing anyone can do. It just... *is*."

His hands stroked across her shoulders, those big warm hands on her skin, sliding intimately over her Lycra tank, curving over the small of her back, and traveling up her spine to the back of her neck. She wanted to lift her face to his neck, to breath him in, to taste his skin, to lick his lips the way she had last night. Craved the pressure of him between her legs, the sizzle of skin on skin.

"Let me take over the expenses here," he murmured, cupping her head and kissing her temple. "I have the money, and you can't keep running these crazy hours. You come here, then you go to cheer practice, then you're at the club until an ungodly hour. You're going to make yourself sick, then where will you be?"

The heat glowing at the center of her body immediately cooled, and she pushed away. "You realize that when you tell me

I can't do something, it just makes me want to prove you wrong, don't you?"

"I didn't mean can't as in *can't*, I just—"

"Mom worked two jobs and raised me for over twenty years. I sure as hell can do it for as long as she needs me. And dammit, there's more to the club than just money. Didn't you hear what I told you last night?"

"I did—"

"I may have taken the job to pay for Mom's care, but I've built it into something different and special.

Something unique. I would still work at the club even if I didn't need the job for Mom."

"I know," he said, gently, seriously. "I talked to the owner last night. He thinks of you like a daughter.

Brags about how much business you've brought in. How much the girls love you. How you're the damn glue that keeps that place together."

She pressed her lips together, not sure how to feel. Or what to believe.

"I don't want to tell you what to do," he said. "I just want you safe and happy. And I want Carolyn comfortable. I love her too."

A mixed flurry of emotion swept in, whirling into chaos. He was able to say he loved her mother but not her. His offer, while sweet and generous, was also ignorant and shortsighted. And the bottom line was...she couldn't depend on him in any way that mattered.

"I know you mean well, Josh, but that's unrealistic in more ways than I have time to explain right now."

He blew out a breath, shifted on his feet, and put his hands on his hips. "What can I do?"

She crossed her arms. "You can leave," she said, in her gentlest voice, even though a sense of loss raged inside her. "Because we both know you've created your life somewhere else, and you're going to leave eventually anyway. It would be better for all of us if you left sooner rather than later."

She opened the driver's door, and Josh caught the top in one big hand. "I'm not leaving like this."

"Like what? Like *this*?" She gestured between them, indicating the conflict brewing. "This is how you left it a year ago. And nothing's changed."

She sat and pulled on the door, but Josh didn't let go. "Everything's changed. And I'm going to find a way to help—both you and Carolyn."

She heaved a sigh, struggling to hold on to her patience while gathering her last whisper of strength to meet his eyes deliberately. "I'm late for cheer practice. Please let go, *I need the money.*"

5

G race pulled her car around to the back of the club, her mind calculating where Josh might be. If he'd left town directly from Safe Haven, he could be waiting on his flight home to Philadelphia. Pushing him away had been heart wrenching, but she had priorities, and he'd chosen not to be among them. She'd just have to find a way to get over it. Eventually, she would. Her mother's Alzheimer's had forced Grace to face a lot of tough times and heartbreaking choices.

She stopped beside the back door, which had been propped open. Drywall leaned against the building, and tools were lined up along the wall.

"Oh jeez," she muttered, glancing around the lot for a work van. "What's broken now?"

She only hoped the cost to fix whatever it was wouldn't interfere with the planned storeroom renovation. Dean had already put her studio on hold once, waiting for his lousy brother-in-law to get his shit together and do the job. Grace had finally convinced him to move forward with a different contractor, but their bids had come in on the high side. Any extra expense or dip in revenue would delay the project again. And she needed that space—one she would lease from Dean to start her own dance school.

Dread snaked down her spine as she pulled the groceries and giant Costco lasagna out of the trunk. She stepped through the back door and scanned the massive dressing room, already buzzing with a dozen dancers pulling out costumes, applying makeup, and styling their hair.

"Hi, ladies," Grace called, her greeting echoed from the others as she set the food down at the other end of the only table, where one of Jasmine's four-year-old twins was sitting, coloring. A mix of African-American and Hispanic, the twins were the most beautiful creatures Grace had ever met. They were also as sweet as sugar and as gregarious as their father. "Hi, Dillon. Where's your mom?"

He looked up with those huge, innocent brown eyes, twirling a blue crayon between his fingers. "Don't know."

Grace nodded at his drawing. "What's that?"

"Transformer. Santa's gonna bring me one for Christmas."

"Cool," she said. "Where's your brother?"

"Helping the builder man."

Grace looked left, toward the storeroom she already considered her dance studio. The double doors were open, and more tools and power cords lay at the threshold. The rattle of a tape measure caught Grace's ear, and she frowned. What the hell could be broken in there?

"Does anyone know where Jasmine is?" Grace asked the room at large. Jasmine was the dancer with the longest history at Allure, and often acted as the house mom when no house mom was around.

"Right here." She came around the corner from the club's main stage. She was the most stunning black woman Grace had ever met, with one of those killer, Amazonian bodies—tall, muscular, and built. She'd pulled her long black braids off her face and wore workout tights and a tank. "Rocco will be here in ten minutes to pick up the boys."

"They're never a problem. I'm worried about whatever's going on back there, though. Please tell me it's not something major like air-conditioning, heating, or plumbing."

"Nothing broken back there, honey." Dillon and Dalton's mother came up beside Grace, and used one perfectly manicured dark hand to lift the aluminum. "What'd you bring us?"

"Lasagna."

"Nice," she sang out, then lowered her voice and turned away from her son. "But not near as nice as the eye candy in the back." She hooked a thumb toward the storeroom, then shook out her hand like it was hot. "Whoo-wee. If I'd known that's who we'd have hanging around here building the studio, I'd have traded days to work all week."

Grace frowned. "Studio?" She glanced that direction again but only heard heavy footsteps and the movement of equipment. No voices. Her mind darted back to the large-bellied contractors who'd been chatting Dean up the night before. "Did Dean approve the bid?" She put a hand to her chest. "Be still my heart."

Jasmine got a devious look in her eye and grinned. "I don't think he's using the same contractors, 'cause the dude back there ain't forty, ain't balding, and his belly has more ridges than a Trojan Ultra Ribbed. And if he's here when the rest of the girls come in tonight, you're gonna have a hard time getting anyone out on stage. You might even have a couple of cat fights over who gets to give him the VIP treatment as a *bonus*." She put air quotes around the last word, then tapped Dillon's shoulder and brought her voice up to a normal level. "Sweet pea, go get your brother. Daddy's gonna be here in a few minutes to take you home."

Dillon set the crayon down and slid off the chair.

"I'll come with you, Dillon," Grace said, patting his soft head of dark curls, still frowning at Jasmine.

"I'd better check out this builder man."

"I don't advise stepping into that room without reflective glasses." She put up her hands and raised her brows. "Just sayin'. Not my fault if your eyeballs fry."

"Jaime, Kaitlin, and Hillary," Grace called, following Dillon as the boy skipped across the dressing room and disappeared through the open double doors, "head out to the stage and start stretching. I'll be right there."

From this angle, Grace could only see one wall of the storeroom, its bare studs now covered with gypsum board. Trepidation crawled through her chest. She was going to be so pissed if Dean had gone for the cheapest labor he could find to—

"Whoa!" The familiar male voice carried from inside the large room, one that made Grace's feet stop midstep. Made her heart flip and squeeze. "What's this? There's *two* of you?"

The twins giggled.

"Good Lord, what a handful," Josh said. "Your poor mother. No, little dude, don't touch that. Here, I'll show you how this works."

An electric buzz filled the air, followed by more giggles from the boys.

Grace didn't know how to respond to his voice. She was first shocked, then angry, then confused, then angry again.

"I'm going to find a way to help—both you and Carolyn."

Josh's last words filled Grace's head.

She pushed her feet forward and gripped the doorframe as she turned into the room, but the sight on the floor in front of her tangled her mind.

Josh knelt on the floor between the twins. He was shirtless, wearing only jeans, lightweight suede work boots, and a leather tool belt. And Grace instantly understood Jasmine's Trojan Ultra

Ribbed metaphor. This wasn't the first time she'd seen his body. Over the years, she'd seen him in swim trunks dozens of times.

But...this was like seeing him again for the first time, all bronze and beefy, the thick muscles of his shoulders and biceps curved and cut. The scars on his right shoulder had healed well, but left thick, discolored welts on his skin. Somehow, it only made him more authentic, more masculine, more...delicious.

"Dillon, Dalton." A strong male voice called from the back door. "Let's go."

The boys ignored their father, enamored with Josh's drill.

"Sounds like Dad's here." Josh put the drill down.

"Noooo," Dalton whined, the twin with hair a shade lighter than the other.

"Again," Dillon chirped, leaning into Josh, half in his lap, hanging on one broad shoulder. "Do it again."

"Little man," Josh said, "I am not gonna get my heinie whooped by your daddy today."

He wrapped an arm around each boy's waist and whipped them up and over his shoulders, one on each side. The boys squealed and giggled, and Josh's smile could have powered the club for a week. But what Grace saw was a wide chest, six-pack abs, and jeans pulled so low by the heavy tool belt that the hollows at his hip bones pointed to what Grace's body craved most.

Jasmine appeared at Grace's side, laughing. "They're going to want to come here after school every day."

"Excuse me, ladies." Josh carried the wiggling bundles of happiness through the doorway, his muscles flexing, then passed through the short hallway toward the rear door where Rocco waited.

Both Grace and Jasmine turned to watch him go. The muscles in his back played in the shadow of the hallway, rippling beneath his tattoo—the skeleton of a frog overlaying a waving American flag, with the word Frogman curved into the design. His ass and thighs filling out his jeans deliciously. Two little boys gigging on his shoulders.

Grace's mind was in the clouds, the only clear thought: *I want that. All that.*

"If your panties haven't melted by now," Jasmine murmured, drawing Grace's mind from the haze, "I might start thinking your sexual preferences have changed."

The comment directed Grace's attention between her legs, where she was hot, tingling, full, aching, and...wet.

"It doesn't matter what's melting," she said, keeping her voice low. "There's way too much bad history between us. And he's way too much like my ex-husband. It's no wonder they were best friends. Isaac always wanted to run things, the same way Josh is trying to run them now. When Isaac came home from overseas, he always expected to get back that sweet twenty-two-year-old kid he'd married. Josh doesn't like me working here. He still treats me like I'm fragile doll." She shook her head and crossed her arms.

"No, I'm not letting my feelings for a man dictate my life ever again. I'm sure as shit not twenty-two anymore."

"Honey, if you don't want to be treated like a kid, act like an adult," Jasmine said in that sassy way of hers, drawing a frown from Grace. "Adults go after what they want, and successful adults do it even when what they want scares them."

Josh's words from the night before pushed into her head. "Damn right you scare me. You're the only thing that's ever scared me, Grace."

She shook her head against the emotional pull the words created. "He's a runner. As soon as his conscience is soothed, he's going to make skid marks out of town."

One of Jasmine's dark eyebrows shot up. "How is that a problem? Girl, you don't have time for the love of your life. Between this job, your cheer jobs, and your mom, you exhaust me—and I parent twin four-year-old maniacs. What you have time for is one smokin' hot guy to hit you up *but good* a few times and then get the hell out of your way."

Grace had never been a hit-and-run kind of girl. But Jasmine was right about one thing—she didn't have any room in her life for the complications of a reciprocal relationship.

Jasmine crossed her arms and leaned her shoulder against the doorjamb. "Go after what you want— *on your terms*. Go after him the same way you're going after this studio. You can be diligently single-minded, girl. Just shift your focus from business to pleasure."

Grace glanced down the hall, where Josh was talking with the twins' father while the boys played at their feet.

A fling? With Josh? That was ridiculous. A disaster waiting to happen. "This has been one *hell* of a long day already." She returned her gaze to Jasmine. "Would you mind telling the girls I'll be right out?"

Josh turned and started back down the hall, grin happy, stride confident.

"I'll tell the girls that you're...indisposed...for the time being." Jasmine passed Josh in the hall on her way back to the dressing room, and punched his shoulder. "If you spoil my boys, they're coming to live with you."

"And I could take you up on that," he said, grinning. "They're great kids. Kudos, Mom."

When he continued toward Grace, Jasmine turned with a hand over her heart and mouthed *oh my God* to Grace before leaving them alone.

All Grace's anger had mellowed into confusion, complicated by all the lust zinging around her body.

"Josh," she said. "This isn't my club. You can't just come in here and start renovating. And this kind of work can't be good for your shoulder."

He put one hand on the wall, one on his hip, and crossed one ankle over the other, all his perfection beautifully on display for Grace. And she was having a hell of a time keeping her gaze on his handsome face.

"I've made all the arrangements necessary with Dean," he said. "And this type of work is exactly what my shoulder needs. Weights give it strength, but this increases mobility, helps develop fine motor movements—something I don't get enough of in my current job."

She crossed her arms, caught between anger and...what? Shock that he'd taken the initiative?

Suspicion that he was working on a project that would only make her work here better, when he'd been clear about not wanting her working here at all? "Isaac told me you're doing consulting work in LA."

"I am," was all he said, adding to Grace's frustration.

She wanted to know about his life, his work. Wanted to know if he was happy. If he ever regretted the move. If he ever missed San Diego. If he ever missed her. Yet, she didn't. "You are... *maddening*."

"I'm good like that." His grin deepened with a sheepish edge. "But hey"—he gestured to the blueprints Grace had paid to have created— "I got the plans from the contractors, and I'm following them to the letter, just the way you wanted."

She shook her head, a hole growing in the pit of her stomach. "Look, I know you want to help, I know you love Mom, and I know—in your own way—you care about me. But I also know what's going to happen here.

"You're going to start this project with a golden heart and great intentions, then leave for Christmas with your family. Then something's going to come up at work, and you're going to leave this half-finished, forcing me to pick up the pieces." She threw her hands out to the sides and let them drop. "I'm sorry,

Josh, but I'm done letting men interfere with my life, take over, and in the end, screw up everything."

Josh's smile evaporated. He exhaled and started toward the doors.

Guilt cut at her heart, but this was self-preservation. She couldn't go back to the way things had always been. "I'm sorry, Josh. I really am."

Instead of walking out, he closed the doors. Then turned and pressed his back there. "You're right.

Beck has spent seven years interfering in your life. I've spent at least three. But when I said everything had changed earlier, I meant it."

Why wasn't she getting through to him? She crossed her arms, failing from keeping her gaze off his torso. It was impossible. He was like a damn sculpture, and she couldn't stop staring. Or wanting. Or aching.

"And I know you've heard that before," he continued. "But this time, I'm going to show you. I'm not going home for Christmas. I've already called my family and told them I won't make it because I have something very important here to take care of."

"You canceled Christmas with your family?" Shock sizzled through her chest. "Josh, *no. No.*"

She lowered her head, closed her eyes, and rubbed her temple. Now she felt guilty. And angry. And grateful. And touched. And so fucking confused.

"I'm spending Christmas here with you and Carolyn and your crew," he said, his voice coming closer.

His hands wrapped her biceps gently. He smelled so completely male, with a touch of sweet sweat and light spice. The hunger inside her gnawed. "And before you accuse me of doing this because I feel guilty, you need to realize there's a difference between caring and obligation. And I care about you, Grace. I know my ways of showing it might feel heavy-handed to you, but that's just me trying to get past your stubbornness.

"I was thinking about what you said earlier, about me picking up the cost for your mom's care not being realistic, and you were right. That's not the answer. You need a steady income for as long as your mom needs to live at the house. Which got me to thinking about what Dean told me—that you want to build this studio and teach from here. And that, I realized, is a perfect idea. I'm just helping it along."

She felt her heart opening. Felt herself falling.

Oh my God, no.

Don't do it.

"Josh, honestly... I appreciate the thought, but it's not healthy for me to have you around."

He released one arm and tilted her chin up so she had to look into his eyes. "I'm going to change that."

Before she could even roll her eyes, his lips touched hers in a gentle, lingering kiss. The action instantly drained all her tension. The release made her lightheaded. Then he kissed her again, and again, a little deeper each time. Her stomach floated. Every reason she had for pushing him away evaporated. And she opened to him.

Josh cupped her face and stroked his tongue into her mouth on a long groan of pure satisfaction that vibrated through her body. The man was an amazing kisser, using his tongue in teasing, tantalizing ways that made Grace think of erotic things, made her body heat and yearn. When she finally pulled away to breathe, she found herself backed against a wall, Josh's muscular body fitted to hers in exquisite perfection.

He tipped his head and kissed her jaw, her throat, her neck, murmuring, "You amaze me, Grace."

His attitude had taken an about-face. She didn't know which way was up anymore.

"I don't have time for this." She breathed the words heavily, needing space to think. "I have to work."

She stepped out from between his body and the wall and tugged at the edge of her top, realizing she still had to change. But she stood there a minute, unable to straighten out her mind enough to get her feet moving.

"What?" Josh finally asked, drawing her gaze.

She shook her head. "I don't know what to do with you."

He smiled, the expression a little smug, a lot sweet, and wrapped his arm around her shoulders as he walked her to the door. Before opening it, he kissed her temple and whispered, "Well, now we've got time to figure that out."

Thirty minutes later Josh pulled his shirt back on and wandered down the hallway toward the club. The sugary female voice echoing through the club sang "Santa Baby"—not exactly what Josh would consider a stripper song. But what the hell did he know?

Grace called out cues above the music. "Remember the eight count, Hillary. Slow down, Jaime.

You've got a beautiful body, let them watch it move. Better. Kaitlin , think sensual. Rock those hips.

Good. Spread your legs, close, spread, close. Pump, pump, pump, sloooow roll... Nice, ladies."

A smile quirked his lips as he passed through the velvet drape toward the club. She was definitely not the woman she'd been a year ago, and, sweet Jesus, she turned him on in wicked ways.

The place was empty except for one girl behind the bar. The younger one...Kati, Kathy... Kelly, that was it. He took a quick glance toward the stage as he hugged the wall, staying in the shadows, but once he caught sight of the stage, his feet stopped.

He couldn't tell exactly what the women were wearing, but it was definitely Santa themed, and minimal. Short red velvet capes rimmed in white feathers covered their bodies, shoulders to hips. Traditional Santa hats adorned their heads. And thigh-high black patent leather spike boots clung to their long legs.

The music stopped, and he continued to the bar, where Kelly unpacked boxes of liquor.

She gave him a flirty, bright grin. "Well, look who's back. What are you up to?"

"Helping Gr—" *Dammit*. "Nikki in the back. Think I could get a beer?"

"Absolutely. What kind?"

"Anything's fine."

On stage, Grace trotted up the stairs, while the girls created a line. She took center stage in front of the other three, wearing the same outfit. The velvet cape hid most of her body, but the long, toned thighs showing between the boot tops and the cape hem gave him plenty to admire.

A bottle clunked against the wooden bar, and Josh pulled out his wallet without ever taking his gaze off Grace.

"On the house." Kelly's voice drew Josh's gaze for a moment. "And this is in case things with you and Nikki don't work out."

She slid a cocktail napkin across the bar—complete with her name, phone number, and x's and o's beneath printed in red ink.

He smiled, nodded, and pocketed the napkin with the intention of throwing it away when she was out of sight. "Thanks."

"Okay, from the top," Grace said as the beginning *ba-bum, ba-bum, ba-bum* of "Santa Baby" spilled through the sound system again.

All four of the women moved forward on the stage in unison, stepping toward the audience, one slow, exaggerated crisscross step per beat. Eartha Kitt's sugary voice filled Josh's ears as he fixed his gaze on Grace. The other three women were undeniably fifteens on a scale of one to ten, but Grace was that and more. She was a powerful, magnetic presence on stage. Absolutely irresistible.

She'd make a mint stripping... Buuuuut, Josh would keep that idea to himself.

The lyrics, *"So hurry down the chimney tonight,"* coincided with the women's twirl and deep bend at the waist, teasing the eye with flaring capes and split-second glimpses of more skin.

Heat stirred in his belly. He definitely needed a better view, one that made it very clear to Grace that he wasn't judging her by where she worked or what she did. He loved what she'd become. It had just taken him a little tap upside the head to realize that.

He picked up his beer and strolled down the center aisle, taking a seat in the front row. Leaning back, he settled into the lushly padded chair, threw his arm over the back of another, and propped his ankle over the opposite knee.

The gazes of all three dancers veered toward him. But not Grace's. She remained perfectly focused, moving to the music and directing the women.

"I'll wait up for you, dear, Santa Baby..."

"Three, four, five and six, seven, shimmy..." she called over Kitt's sugar-soft voice, which sounded far more erotic now than when he'd first heard it.

All four women rocked their shoulders, and the capes fell in unison to their elbows, exposing bare, smooth chests, and jiggling breasts barely contained in red corsets edged in white fur.

Holy mother of God...

Heat flooded Josh's veins and pooled between his legs. Pressure built in his chest until he wanted to moan with it.

The women leaning back in a provocative stance, rolling

their upper bodies like an ocean wave. But Josh had frozen, hand locked around the beer bottle, throat tight.

Grace strutted across the stage in those fuck-me boots with a swish, swish, swish of hips, swinging the cape.

"Five and six, seven and drop," she instructed the women on another turn, another kick, and the capes fell to the floor, exposing the outfit hidden beneath.

And *Lord help him,* he couldn't form one thought. Not one fucking coherent thought .

All he could see was Grace. Her red corset laced up the front, cleavage showing through the V. The fur trim barely covered her nipples. Her breasts spilled over the top, bouncing with every move. Her skirt rode a good five inches beneath her flat belly button, the fabric accented with a wide black patent leather belt to match the boots, and exposed every inch of trim, toned, shapely torso from hip bones to rib cage.

"And roll...roll...roll..." Grace was saying, but Josh had lost track of the choreography.

This was beyond his hottest sexual fantasy. She was gorgeous, sensual, erotic, naughty, and sweet all at the same time. Everything a man could ever want all packaged inside a generous, compassionate, resilient woman.

Every turn, flip, or twist flashed the hint of a red lace thong beneath the skirt's white fur trim. Every slow, sultry bend exposed her tight ass cheeks—completely bare but for a tiny strip of red lace disappearing between the golden curves.

A sharp spin turned all four women away from Josh as they strutted to the rear of the stage. Their black boots crisscrossed, their hips swayed. Then they all stopped abruptly, and on the next burst of orchestra music, all four women ripped their bodices open with both hands.

"Whoa," he murmured, riveted to the power of such tight choreography between dance and music. But that thought skipped from his mind when they turned back toward the audience, exposing tiny, tiny, *tiny* red bikini tops. And as they strutted forward, all Josh saw were Grace's perfect breasts, plump and high and deliciously mobile in a triangle of red. He wanted them in his hands again, beneath his tongue again.

He swallowed hard, his throat so dry the movement hurt. On their way to the front of the stage, they dropped the corsets to the floor. The fingers of his free hand dug into his thigh. His cock rubbed uncomfortably against his jeans, and his chest felt as tight as if he were wearing a corset of his own.

Josh dragged his gaze up Grace's body—and found her gaze directly, purposefully on his. The sight speared his body with heat, the reaction so visceral she could have been reaching between his legs and cupping his balls.

Then she grabbed one of the gold stripper poles, hiked herself up with one hand in an effortless, smooth move that reminded Josh of the way she'd lifted her body up his the night before, and twirled slowly to the floor, still calling out direction.

"Spin, spin, spin, reach, pull..." Her words mirrored her spiral down the pole, her reach into her hair, her pull of whatever had been holding it up, and the sleek strands spilled in a copper waterfall.

When she reached the floor, her legs spread in an artful, erotic split around the pole, exposing her sex, barely hidden by a scrap of red lace. And her blue-eyed gaze kept drawing his own back. Back to eyes that screamed *I'm strong and confident and I can take care of myself*.

And Josh was blown away by her skill, her strength, her professionalism, but even more by how motherfucking *hot* she made him.

She strutted away, bent at the waist, and exposed her ass before performing some insanely dirty crawl across the stage that made Josh want to pop out of his jeans. The need to reach between his legs and stroke himself simply to relieve the pressure had one hand clenched around the arm of the chair, the other around his beer bottle. That was when he realized he'd hit his limit. Every muscle in his body screamed with tension, needing release.

As Grace gripped the stripper pole and flung her body upside down, spread her legs, and slowly spiraled to the floor with her gaze hot and unwavering on his, Josh hit his sexual-eye-candy limit and forced himself to stand. Forced himself to turn. Forced himself to put one foot in front of the other in a physically, mentally, and emotionally excruciating stride away from the stage.

6

Grace was breathing hard when the song ended for the seventh time. She pulled herself off the floor and gathered the garments she'd torn off during the dance—not as many as the other girls, but enough to give Josh a great view.

At first, she'd thought him watching her semistrip would turn him off, which she'd convinced herself was better for both of them. Then, as he'd watched her dance, his expression had shifted from skeptic-laced curiosity to white-hot, I-wanna-do-you-fast-and-hard-up-against-a–wall-right-fucking-now.

But, in the end, he'd walked out.

Story of her life, right?

Feeling confused, she descended the stairs with the club staff buzzing around, preparing for the doors to open. Hillary, Jaime, and Kaitlin had disappeared into the dressing room, but just as Grace was about to pass through the drape and into the hallway, Jasmine popped through, already decked out in her outfit for the opening dance.

"Hey," Grace said. "Something wrong?"

Jasmine crossed her arms. "You tell me. I was coming to see

just what you were doing out here to turn the mighty navy SEAL into an overheated, tongue-tied mess of nerves."

Grace lifted a brow.

"He came back there red-faced and sweating, with his jeans sporting a bulge as big as a football. Then he tripped over the threshold on his way out the back door, where he stuck his head under the hose."

She frowned hard. "Is he sick?"

"Yeah, honey." Jasmine snorted a laugh. "I think it's called Semen Retention Syndrome. Also known as blue balls."

"Yeah?" she asked, still unsure.

"Hell, yeah."

Grace's worry drained, and a smile quirked her mouth. "Now he knows how I've felt all these years."

Jasmine turned Grace toward the hallway by the shoulder and gave her a gentle push. "Get back there and negotiate some relief for both of you." She started toward the bar. "I've got to go bribe—I mean *negotiate*—with the staff for the night."

Grace's heels clicked on the cement and echoed off the walls as she strode down the hall. In the back, the girls buzzed around the dressing room, gossiping, laughing, and bitching like always.

She found the back door standing open, but the grind of a power saw drew her gaze toward the storeroom. He hadn't walked out. He was—in his self-described, heavy-handed way— showing her he cared.

As the staff tested the sound system, the muffled boom of music hummed through the walls. She wandered to an empty dressing table in a corner and picked up the padded chair. As an afterthought, she opened one of the drawers and slipped out an Allure condom—also used as business cards, with the dancer's stage name imprinted on one side and the club name printed on the other—from the box there. In this case, it didn't matter whose name resided on the foil. If Grace didn't use it, the promo goodie would return to the drawer.

Looking at the shiny silver package in her palm made her think about Josh getting hard. Made her think about taking his rigid, hot cock in her hand. Made her think about stroking the condom on. And, ultimately, feeling him slide deep inside her.

Her whole body responded to the instantaneous fantasy—muscles tight, temperature rising, pussy aching.

Shrugging into her velvet cape, she tucked the foil square into the waistband at her hip and carried the chair toward the storeroom.

She wandered in and glanced over the hills and valleys of muscle along Josh's back. He'd taken off his shirt again—praise the gods—and was leaning over a piece of gypsum board, guiding a circular saw through the sheet. A small plume of white billowed behind the saw, and a fine white mist coated his skin.

He finished the cut, turned off the saw, and glanced up. Through the clear goggles, his eyes widened, slipped down her body, then slid away.

"Hey." He pulled the goggles off and set them on the board, then gestured to the one strip of mirror he'd placed on the longest wall. "I just put a piece of the glass up for you to see before I went on. And I need to know how high you want the dance bar." His gaze turned to the plans. "After seeing how flexible you are, I think the height called out in here is too low."

She strolled in, set the chair down facing Josh, and, still standing, bent at the waist and crossed her arms on the curved back. The move made her breasts fall forward and the cape drape open. "I couldn't care less about the bar's height at the moment."

His gaze darted up, immediately lowered from her face to her chest, and slid away again, but not before the fiery burst of lust lit them from within. He cleared his throat. Licked his lips. Turned his back to her. "We can talk about it after you change."

He wanted her. Not only could she see it in his expression and hear it in the tone of his voice, she felt it in the air—a crackling, thick, hot desire filling the room. She turned and slowly strode to the doors, but instead of leaving, she closed them. Then turned the dead bolt and pressed her back against the wood.

Josh turned with a look of confusion. But as soon as his eyes met hers, a nervous tic pulled at the skin beneath his left eye.

She'd only seen Josh nervous once in all the years they'd known each other—when she'd asked him to move in with her while he recovered from shoulder surgery. The expression he'd had then was the same one he had now, one that said, I-want-that- *but...*

With determination fueling her steps, Grace started a slow, sexy walk toward him, extending her legs, crisscrossing her boots, holding the I-want-to-fuck-you sultry look she constantly required of the dancers.

"You left before the number was over." She laid her hand on the gypsum board, toying with the edge with one finger. "Missed the best part of the show."

He was fighting to keep his gaze on her face, but it kept slipping, and the heat there deepened. "If that's true," he said, his voice low and rough, "I'm glad I left when I did, or I would have definitely embarrassed myself."

She stepped close and purposely met and held his gaze as she pressed the tip of her index finger to the center of his chest. "So...you didn't hate it."

She let her gaze follow her finger as she drew the tip upward along his sternum. The barely there white mist cleared to show tanned skin beneath. Then she arched to the left, creating a curve around the top of his pec muscle and dragged her finger down at an angle sharp enough to brush his nipple as she passed.

The nub hardened beneath her finger, and Josh sipped a little breath of surprise. She continued in a slow, downward angle until her finger touched the waistband of his jeans. And, yes, there was definitely a substantial bulge there. One she desperately wanted to explore.

"Seeing me dance like that doesn't...I don't know...disgust you on any level?"

She scraped her lower lip between her teeth and placed the tip of her finger at the original starting point. Then followed her previous pattern, this time, arcing to the right.

"The opposite," he murmured, voice rough. "Seeing you own that stage is ridiculously hot."

Her smile deepened, her confidence soared, and with it, her lust broke free, spilling through her body like glitter.

This time when she brushed his opposite nipple, gooseflesh broke out over his chest, and his eyes closed for a brief second. She finished off the nearly invisible shape of a heart where her finger met his jeans again. Fisting the waistband, she pulled him around so his back faced the chair, then pushed him into the seat.

His breath whooshed out on a soft grunt. Before he could speak, Grace planted her heel on the seat at his hip, gripped his face in both hands, and leaned in until her mouth was a breath from his and whispered, "I'm about ready to own *you*."

Instead of kissing him, she stroked his bottom lip with her tongue. He opened and leaned forward, his mouth searching for hers, but she pulled back with a teasing smile. "On my terms."

This power trip was a surge of lusty goodness, and she wondered if this was how the dancers felt on stage in front of dozens of men. She took two steps back, shrugged the cape, and let it fall to her elbows.

The throb of Korn's grungy beat of "Coming Undone" pulsed through the walls, and her body moved easily, smoothly, and without any conscious thought. For Grace, dancing was built into her muscle memory. What she needed to concentrate on now was tantalizing Josh out of his mind.

Turning her back to him, she let the cape slide off her arms, let her upper body fall forward, exposing her ass beneath the short little skirt for Josh's view—just out of his reach.

"Jesus—" he rasped, but trailed off when she straightened, tossed her hair back, and rocked her hips in a slow sway as she lowered to a crouch, thighs spread.

She fell to her knees, then her belly. Rolled and sat up, letting her hands stroke up her body to the beat of the muffled music.

Josh was leaning forward, elbows on knees. Lids heavy, eyes burning, skin glistening with a fresh sweat. "You're killin' me, Grace."

When he held out his hand, she took it, easing to her feet, but when he tried to pull her close, she spun out of reach and strode behind him. One hand slid across his wide shoulders, before she leaned in, pressing her breasts to his back, but the small amount of skin-on-skin contact wasn't near what she needed. She kissed his neck. He was salty and gritty, smelling of sawdust and fresh sweat and lust. He was everything she craved.

Her hands trailed across his shoulders, over his hard chest, down his warm abdomen. His hands covered her arms, caressed her skin. He dropped his head back, and pressed his face to the base of her neck just as her hand slid over his crotch.

Heat and sensation spread outward from his mouth, slid into her chest, and pulled at her nipples. She tightened her hand on his cock, hard and thick beneath his jeans.

His mouth dropped open on a groan, and his hands rose to grip her face and pull her mouth to his—open and hot. His tongue swept in, found hers, and stroked. She met his kiss and returned all the passion as her fingers worked his button, pulled at his zipper, pushed at fabric, and finally, *finally* closed around his bare cock.

Josh broke the kiss on a rough "Ah, *fuck*..." His hips lifted into her touch. "Gracie..."

Her name was a plea. One that exposed his need, his vulnerability. Grace fed off each and every reaction, gaining a sense of power, of control, of possession—but not over Josh. Over herself. That combined with living out this fantasy was absolutely intoxicating.

She pulled the condom from her waistband, held it in front of him so he could watch her tear the foil and unroll the slick coil just enough to swallow his head, then scraped his ear between her teeth and whispered, "I'm so wet for you."

"Holy fuck..." He was panting now, muscles strung tight, one hand gripping the edge of the chair, one arm up and around her neck, his hand fisted in her hair. His gaze followed her hands as she pulled his cock from the restriction of his boxers and stroked him, loving the feel of the silky smooth skin covering a steel-hard cock. "Gracie..."

She fitted the condom to the head of his cock.

His hips pulsed on a curse. His head fell back, mouth dropped open, eyes squeezed tight. "*Fuck*." His head rolled side to side, and the hand on the chair snapped up and gripped her wrist, pulling her hand from him. "I can't... I'm sorry. It's been too long. I can't have you touching me like that. I need to be inside you when I come, Grace. *Need to.*"

She kissed his neck. Once, twice, three times, until his hand relaxed around her wrist. "I'm on board,"

she whispered, "but let me get this on first."

And she stroked the condom down his length. His muscles contracted, hips lunged, back arched.

A low, hot laugh slipped from her throat, a thrill rolling through her veins. "Damn, this is fun."

He clamped down on her wrist and hauled her around the chair, wrapping his forearm around her waist as he tried to pull her onto his lap. "This is more fun."

"You forgot something." Grace pushed against his shoulders and wiggled away. Standing in front of him in full fluorescent light, Grace bent, laid her hands against her knees, then dragged them slowly up her thighs, lifting her skirt. Josh's gaze burned over the red thong, his chest rising and falling with shallow, quick breaths. "These might get in the way."

She hooked her thumbs into the panties at her hips and shimmied them down until her skirt covered her pussy again, then she let her panties drop down her thighs, her calves. Pressing one hand to the seat beside Josh's hip, she bent provocatively over his lap while reaching for her panties and dragging them over her heels.

Josh sat forward, both hands gripping the backs of her thighs, sliding higher, higher, then cupping her ass. Big, warm, firm hands squeezing her cheeks.

"Fucking perfect," he murmured, tugging her closer.

She caught herself with one hand on the back of the chair. Josh's hands slid back down her thigh and lifted her thigh to his hip. Then his fingers stroked the heat between her legs from behind, and a luscious wave of pleasure rocked through her sex, her hips, her chest.

She arched, pushing her pussy back, and her breasts forward. Suddenly, she was totally out of control again. Josh's thick fingers touched and stroked, while his other hand gripped her breast, shoved the tiny bikini top aside, and he sucked her nipple into his mouth.

"Oh *God*..." She arched higher, and Josh pushed his fingers into her heat.

He groaned against her breast, licking and sucking her nipple while his other hand created a whirlwind of delicious pressure in her pussy. Time and place started to slip away. The music faded against the siren rising in her head. It had been so long. So very, very long. He did everything too right. And it was coming too fast.

"Josh..." she panted, gripping the chair so tight her hand had gone numb. Glancing down, she found his eyes closed, long golden lashes soft against his cheek, an expression of bliss on his face, that sexy mouth covering her breast again and again. "Josh...I can't..."

As if knowing she was trying to tell him she couldn't wait, he pushed deep into her body and...did something...exquisite. Something that made the razor edge of heaven streak through her body, made her mouth drop, made her throat close around a scream of ecstasy.

Then he scraped his teeth over her nipple and she felt the bite all the way to her pussy, shooting her over the edge.

"Fuck, fuck, *fuck*..." The orgasm hit her so hard, her body jerked and she fell forward. Josh caught her around the waist and held her tight as the orgasm ripped through her body in shards of pleasure and light.

Smaller pleasure shocks rippled through her, pussy clenching, clit tingling, belly quivering.

She hadn't even found the strength to open her eyes, when Josh gripped her waist, lifted her off the ground and drew her over his lap.

Her knee caught on the edge of the chair, and Josh hauled it free, dragging her thighs to straddle his own. "Sorry, fuck... Can't wait... Jesus, Grace... Look at me, baby." With one hand positioning his cock against her slick sex, he gripped her face with the other and dragged her gaze to his. "Look at me."

As soon as her heavy-lidded eyes latched on to his, he lifted, pressing the head of his cock past the tightness of her entrance. The stretch, the burn, the pressure—it was exquisite, and Grace closed her eyes on a sound between a moan and a cry.

Josh froze. His hand tightened on her face. "Grace?"

"So good," she panted. "Don't stop."

"Jesus..." His muscles uncoiled, and he shoved her skirt up, fisted it against her hip as he lowered her in excruciatingly slow increments onto his cock. But he was thick, and long and by the time she surrounded him, they were both dripping sweat. "Fuck, baby, you're so damn tight."

She tried to smile but half winced instead. "I don't get out much."

"That's insane." He kissed her lips. "You're so hot, so gorgeous..." He kissed her neck, giving her time to adjust to his size. "*God*, you feel *so fucking good*..."

"Man," she laughed, tipping her head, giving him room to slide his mouth to her collarbone. "You're a talker..."

"I've wanted this for so fucking long..."

"Then let's get this show started." She tipped her head, kissed his lips, and whispered, "Hook your feet on the chair rungs, and hold on for the ride."

Josh's thighs tensed beneath her as he repositioned his boots, and she met his gaze, stroking her hands up her body and sweeping her bikini top off over her head. Josh's hungry eyes fell to her breasts. She continued to slide her hands around her neck, beneath her hair, and collected the silky mass into messy handfuls.

Then she started to move. She didn't know if this rhythm came naturally to all women or if her dancing made it feel so perfect, but dragging his thick cock against her walls and driving him back in until the pressure tugged on her clit and spread pressure through her pelvis felt beautiful and perfect and as primal as breathing.

"You are more woman than I ever dreamed of." His hands traveled over her body, his gaze following.

"Sexier than my hottest fantasy."

Her second orgasm built fast and deep, a push of pleasure every time she sank over him. She gripped the back of the chair and used her thighs to pump harder, faster.

Josh's hands cupped her head, drawing his mouth to hers, where his kiss was erotic and loose and wet, just like their sex. Then he broke away his hands sliding over her breasts, pinching her nipples, shooting twin shocks of pleasure straight between her legs. He gripped her waist, his big, rough hands spanning across smooth, delicate skin, and drew her down on his cock harder while lifting into her.

The head of his cock hit that place deep, deep inside her that squirted pleasure through her body, and she moaned.

"You like it hard?"

"Hard and deep. I can't get enough."

Josh leveraged the rungs of the chair. His thighs, rock hard and warm, clenched on every upward thrust. His hands pulled her hips down to meet him.

"Oh *shit*, yes," she breathed, her chest inflating with another climax. "God, perfect." Another slam, and she whimpered at the extreme perfection of it. "Don't stop. Please don't stop."

His thrusts grew faster, creating a perfect rhythm. "Look at me, Gracie."

She opened heavy lids and found a level of heat in his gaze she couldn't ever remember seeing in any man, not even Isaac. Josh was focused, intense, determined. And she realized she wasn't owning him, he was owning her.

And that was exactly what she wanted—to be his.

She released the chair with one hand, cupped his face, and pressed her forehead to his.

"Come for me again, Gracie," he ordered more than asked. Pounding, pounding, pounding. "Come for me."

This orgasm hit like a punch of velvet, harder and deeper and longer than the first, arching her back and rocking her body. Josh's muscles turned to rock beneath her, his guttural sounds vibrating against the skin of her neck as he broke, hips pumping, hands digging into her hips.

Then he suddenly relaxed, slumping in the chair, dropping his head back, releasing her body to drop his arms out to the sides. Breathing hard, he closed his eyes, his face utterly lax, sweat dripping from his temple. He stretched his legs out with a groan, and the muscles rocked beneath her.

"Don't...move..." he said between pants. "Let me...find my...brain..."

Grace smiled, her forehead resting on his shoulder. Her body felt loose and tingly and amazing. And her heart hurt— but in a good way, stretched full and aching with so much love she didn't know what to do with it all.

A knock sounded on the door. "Nikki? Charlotte needs you. Her costume ripped, and she goes on in ten."

She groaned, lifted her head, and called, "Be right out."

Then put her head back down and snuggled closer to Josh. He chuckled, the sound deep and satisfied.

His arms slid around her, one stroking her back, the other her hair. She wanted to sink in and fall asleep with him like this. The blissful thought made her smile, but knowing he'd be leaving soon turned the sensation bittersweet.

"Before you get all caught up in the vortex waiting for you out there," his voice rumbled near her ear,

"let me just tell you that was the very best sex ever. Like... *ever*."

Sex. Yep, that was what she'd planned. That was what she'd delivered. And it was still all they could have.

Now, she just had to figure out what to do with all these emotions left over.

"Amazing." She kissed his neck. "I knew it would be." The pinch of reality crept in, and she forced her head from his shoulder. "Guess the fun and games are over, though."

She pushed up on her knees, easing him from her body with a laughing groan. He helped her to her feet and said, "Throw me one of those rags, baby, would you?"

Crouching to pick up her panties, bikini, and cape on the way, she plucked up a clean white rag and tossed it to him. While he cleaned up, she shook the white dust off her clothes and redressed.

Josh stood, zipped his pants, then swayed and gripped the chair for balance. "Whoa. All my blood must still be a little too far south."

She chuckled and moved languidly up behind him, and laid a hand on his sweaty back.

He turned, swept her close, and kissed her. Then slowly pulled out of the kiss with "Stay with me tonight?"

Oh. That she hadn't expected. Flashes of intimacy ticked through her mind, and a sizzle of fear coursed along her ribs. She didn't need any more reasons to fall deeper in love with him. Not when he'd be gone in a matter of days.

"I'm going to be here late," she said with a casual smile. Better to keep this light. "And I've got six a.m. cheer practice."

Another knock on the door. "Nikki? Charlotte's on in five, and she's getting panicky."

Grace pushed up on her toes and gave him a soft, sweet, but chaste we're-done kiss. "See you tomorrow?"

"Absolutely." He smiled, but she saw the disappointment in his eyes.

She knew she looked like she'd just been fucked silly in a room full of white dust, but she didn't care.

And the fact that she wasn't ashamed for going after the best sex of her life with the only man she'd ever truly loved gave her a sense of complete freedom. Maybe for the first time in her life.

At the door, she turned the lock and pulled the door open a few inches, then glanced back and found him watching, his expression veiled now, but a lost sense of confusion hung around him. The urge to console him gnawed at her, but considering who he was, she knew that was impossible. Giving him the night to come to the same realization was best for them both.

7

J osh stood at the front door of Safe Haven the following evening holding a bag of craft supplies that should have lightened his mood. But the unease that had gnawed at him all day remained.

By the time Grace had finished cheer practice and gotten to the club, the place was buzzing with activity. She'd barely had time to shoot him a smile and a "Hey, how's it going?" before she'd been swept up in the vortex of schedules, music choices, costumes, and dance routines.

And their lack of communication after what they'd shared the night before had left him feeling insecure and disconnected. He didn't want their encounter to become a one-time, casual, off-the-cuff fluke, and he was afraid that was exactly how Grace had seen it.

He shook the worried thought from his head and knocked, hoping spending some time with Carolyn would preoccupy him for a few hours while Grace was working.

Tammy greeted him with her typical enthusiasm and led him through the living room and into the great room, where he found Carolyn snug in a lounge chair with ear buds in.

"I don't want to disturb her," he said, pausing just inside the archway.

The great room had been turned into a Christmas wonderland, and smelled like a pine forest. A live, twenty-five-foot noble fir reached into the cathedral ceilings, twinkling with multicolored lights and glistening with tinsel. Figurines decorated every horizontal surface, more presents had been stuffed beneath the tree.

"Nonsense." Tammy urged him forward by the arm. "She's had a really good day. This is the best time to visit. I just wish Grace could spend some time with her today."

Tammy rubbed her hand on Carolyn's shin to get her attention. Her eyes opened, then focused on her caretaker, and Carolyn smiled, one of those warm, comfortable smiles. She reached up to take a headphone from her ear when her gaze darted to Josh, and she paused.

His gut tightened. He didn't want his presence to spark another setback for her.

Slowly, her smile broadened. "My Lord, Josh? Is that you?"

Relief eased his shoulders. "Hey, Carolyn."

He leaned down, gave her a one-armed hug, and kissed her cheek. She smelled of soft perfume and powder.

She wrapped her arms around his neck. "Oh, son, how are you? It's been so long. How's the shoulder?"

Jesus, she remembered? He was still reeling from her remembering him at all.

"Better. Much better." He pulled back and crouched beside her chair. Her eyes were watery with emotion, and she stroked his face with a cool, frail hand. "You look amazing."

"Aw, you're sweet," she said, patting his cheek. "Is Gracie here too?"

"She couldn't get away from work tonight."

"That little girl." Carolyn lowered her hand. "She works so

hard. I wish...I wish I could have done more to make her life easier."

"She seems pretty darn happy." Josh covered her hand with his and squeezed. "And you're a great mom."

Her smile softened. "Gracie will be better. She's going to make an amazing mother."

Grace. A mother. The idea warmed a place deep in his belly. Why hadn't he ever thought of that before? "I'm sure she will. She learned from the best."

A smile of gratitude fluttered over her lips. If Josh hadn't seen Carolyn lose it yesterday, he wouldn't believe she needed to be in a home. She was completely lucid and sharp, her blue eyes watery but direct.

"Isaac should have given her a baby," she said. "If he had, they might still be together."

Josh's mind drifted backward. Whenever he'd brought up the subject of children to Beck, his teammate brushed it off, telling him Grace wasn't ready. "Did she want one?"

Carolyn laughed softly, her expression filled with love. "Oh, yes. From the moment she and Isaac got serious. And then, even more when he was gone so much." Carolyn shook her head, her gaze going distant again. "She was so terribly lonely. She had me, but I was always working or tired. A baby would have been such a beautiful addition to her life. In Grace's eyes, the sun would have risen and set on her child.

But Isaac..." She shook her head, then shrugged.

Beck was selfish. Josh didn't need Carolyn to tell him that; he knew. But Beck also *had* to be selfish.

He was a warrior. His mission in life was to protect his country. Any other mission diluted focus. And there was no room for straying focus as a SEAL. Josh had been selfish during those years too—it was the very reason he hadn't asked Grace out when he, Beck, and the rest of the team had met her at a restaurant where she'd been waitressing. But Beck hadn't had the same reservations.

Tammy, who'd been standing by, patted Josh's shoulder. "Looks like you have everything under control. Enjoy your time. I'll be in the kitchen if you need me."

Josh nodded, then returned his gaze to Carolyn. "So, how are you feeling?" He lifted the brown bag and smiled. "Up to a little project?"

"Oh..." She clapped her hands in front of her chest. "You know how I love crafting."

"I do. And I'm also hoping you still love butterflies."

She gasped, her eyes sparkling like a kid's. "I *love* butterflies."

He pushed to his feet, held the bag under his arm, and offered her both hands. "We'll need to sit at a table."

"This is so fun. I wish Gracie could be here. She loves craft projects."

The little seductress loved crafts, huh? Josh grinned and tucked that nugget away for later use—something more along the lines of edible body paint.

He helped Carolyn to the table and pulled a chair up under her, then turned the bag over, spilling all the supplies he'd bought earlier that day across the table. "Any guesses yet?"

"Oh..." Her eyes lifted to Josh's. "A suncatcher?"

"Bingo."

Her fingers shifted through the large black butterfly foam shape and the rainbow of tissue paper.

"Josh... You're such a sweet boy." She smiled at him sadly. "I know you must miss your team, your work as a SEAL, but Grace and I missed you so much when you were gone."

He pulled a chair up to the table and clasped his hand over hers again. "I appreciated every letter, every package you sent. You know that, don't you?"

"Of course. Thank you, sweetheart."

"One of my favorites was the one you sent right before my accident. Which is why I chose this project for tonight."

"I'm sorry, son." She looked a little worried. "I don't remember what package you're talking about."

"How could you?" he said, making light of her memory lapse. "You sent so many, there's no way you could keep track. It was a box of different suncatchers you'd made with your second graders, who donated them to our team."

She raised her brows, and Josh could see her searching her memory with no luck. As he set up the craft, spreading out newspaper and lining up all the supplies, he said, "Each kid made a different design.

So I hung the turtle in Dunlap's room, because he's always late."

That made Carolyn laugh, and the distress in her eyes eased.

"And I gave the elephant to Ghost, because he's got that damned photographic memory. The rooster went to Decker, because he's just a..."

Ooops.

"Prick?" she supplied with a sly little grin.

Humor tickled his insides, and he burst out laughing. Carolyn joined in. Josh hadn't felt this good in so long. "And I gave the octopus to Joey, because he's such a—"

"Pussy," she finished.

"And the peacock to—"

"Had to have been Bobby," she said. "He liked to strut his stuff for the ladies."

"How'd you know that? He was always on his best behavior unless he was alone with the guys."

"Not always." She smiled down at the colorful paper. "I heard about his antics at the diner where Grace used to work."

Josh chuckled, remembering how Bobby's crude pickup line had backfired on him. "She told you about the pickle?"

Carolyn's brow creased, and she gave Josh a curious grin. "Remind me."

"So, Bobby ordered a burger. Grace told him the restaurant makes the best pickles in the county and asked if he'd like one on the side. Bobby comes back with 'I've already got a great pickle, honey, but I'd be willing to share it with you.'

"Without a second's pause, Grace wrinkles her nose but keeps her voice sugary sweet and says, 'No, thanks. All *those* pickles get canned around here.'"

CAROLYN'S LAUGH was rich and flowing, and the sound seemed to sparkle through Josh's chest. "That's my girl."

Josh squeezed Carolyn's hand. "I've missed you."

"I've missed you too, but Grace has missed you most."

Guilt bubbled up again, and after everything he'd discovered over the last two days, he wondered if it would ever clear. He'd been wrong to leave her last year. Wrong to stay away. When it came to Grace, he'd been just as selfish as Beck. Doing it for the right reasons didn't make the hurt feel any different.

"She hasn't been the same since you left," Carolyn continued. "Oh, she's good at pretending.

Everything's fine, Mom. I love my job, Mom. I don't need a man in my life, Mom. But I know my girl.

Just because my memory slips now and then doesn't mean I can't still read her—or you—when all my marbles are clanking around this old jar."

She knocked her fist against her skull, making Josh smile.

"Well, I'm hoping to convince her to let me stay around now."

Carolyn searched his eyes for what felt like an eternity. "Do you love her, Josh? I mean *really* love her, not the way Isaac loved her."

His stomach clenched. "How did Isaac love her?"

"As an afterthought." Her steady, open gaze speared Josh's heart. "Grace is a beautiful soul. She deserves to be treasured, not abandoned."

"I agree," he said. "And, yes, Carolyn, I *really* love her."

Grace pulled up to Safe Haven, and her headlights shone on the trunk of Josh's white Lexus sedan. She sat there, car running, frown deepening, unable to wrap her mind around his presence here. Her thoughts immediately darted to the negative—that there must have been a problem with her mother and Tammy hadn't been able to get hold of her, so they'd called Josh.

She was out of the car and halfway to the door before common sense returned, and she realized that didn't make any sense.

On the way up the walk, she glanced into the great room, the lights inside creating a fish bowl effect in the dark night. She saw Josh's blond head first, then pushed up on her tiptoes and found her mother sitting at a table with him. And she was smiling.

Smiling.

Grace hadn't seen her mother smile in months.

With her heart tripping over itself, she hurried to the door, gave a cursory knock, and walked in.

Tammy met her in the foyer.

"Is everything okay?" Grace asked.

"It's great. I'm so glad you could come. She's having a wonderful day. Just like her old self. And she's really enjoying Josh's company."

Grace's gaze snapped back to Tammy from the direction of the great room. "She knows him?"

"Recognized him the minute he walked in," Tammy said, beaming.

Grace pulled in a sharp breath and tented her fingers over her nose and mouth. Hope and happiness over the small change made her chest feel full and tight.

"He's a positive trigger," Tammy said. "Maybe that's what she needed to get out of the funk she went through after Betty died."

Josh had been a positive trigger in Grace's life too.

"How long has he been here?" she asked.

Tammy glanced at her watch. "About an hour."

"And she's been lucid this whole time?"

"The whole time. They've been chattering like little girls," she teased. "But I can tell she's getting tired. Don't be surprised if she slips a little."

Grace nodded, squeezed Tammy's arm in gratitude, and walked into the great room, her chest fizzing with anticipation. Josh sat with his back toward the doorway, but her mother looked over as she came in.

Grace stopped in her tracks, shoulders tight, breath suspended.

Recognition sparked in her mother's eyes, and her face brightened into a smile. "Gracie, you made it."

Gracie. She hadn't heard her mother say her name for so long, the word felt like a sweet stroke of her hand. Loss and love mixed, wrapping around Grace's heart and freezing her in place.

"Oh, my, don't you look beautiful?" Carolyn said. "What a pretty little dress. Come help with this project Josh brought. Look."

She'd changed from her seductive, revealing work dress into one of her everyday simple knee-length flowy sheaths for the visit, but her mother's mind was back on her project, lifting the black outline of a butterfly, its body and wings striped in colored tissue paper.

Josh stood and started toward her but paused a few feet

away, his expression concerned. "Are you...okay? You look...
Shit, are you mad?"

"Mad?" She didn't understand the question.

"That I came to see her without telling you?" He took
another step closer. "You were so busy, and I've gone as far as I
can with the studio until the flooring comes in. I didn't think
you'd have time to get over to see your mom, so..."

A rough laugh bubbled from her chest. "So *you* came? And
you brought *butterflies*?"

His brows pulled. His expression shifted from worried to
defensive as he shoved his hands into his pockets. "She likes
butterflies."

"I know." She laughed the words, but they sounded as mysti-
fied as she felt. "I guess I'm just...I don't know...shocked. You
come to visit her with time you don't have, while here doing a
favor for a friend, who also happens to be her own ex-son-in-
law. An ex-son-in-law who has never so much as called her since
she's been here. Would never even consider visiting her here.
And who sure as hell *never* had any clue she likes butterflies."

Josh angled his head. "So...I still can't tell if you're angry with
me or not, but...are you telling me that Beck knows your mother's living here? He knows that she has...this problem?"

The change of topic drained Grace's sense of wonder. "He
knows," she said, forcing her anger toward Isaac away so she
could appreciate what she had right now—a mother who recognized her and a man who truly cared about them both. "He
knows everything. And I'm not angry—not at you."

She slid her hand down Josh's arm and tugged one of his
hands from his pocket, then threaded their fingers together.

"She hasn't called me Gracie for months." She smiled up at him, not caring that her eyes had to be watery with tears. "Thank you."

He exhaled, and his shoulders relaxed. But his gaze went hot and intense. "I want to kiss you so badly right now."

She scraped her lower lip between her teeth. "I could probably find a way to satisfy that craving."

"Soon, I hope."

"Maybe."

The doubt cleared from his eyes, and he grinned. "Such a tease."

"You love it."

"*Hell* yes."

"Oooooh, look." Her mother's excited coo drew both their gazes, and she held up another suncatcher, this one with tracing paper in shades of blue and green. "This will match Henrietta's new bedspread."

Grace turned, her hand still in Josh's, and they walked to the table. "Are you two making them for the whole house?"

"Three done, three to..." Her gaze caught on their joined hands, and her words trailed off with a look of confusion. Grace's chest burned with that guilty-teenager sensation, and she drew her hand from Josh's and took a seat next to her mom, hoping that hadn't tipped her mother off balance.

"So you've had a good day?" Grace said. "You look so pretty tonight. Did Tammy do your hair this morning?"

Her mother nodded, setting the butterfly aside with a familiar distance in her eyes. Then she slanted an odd grin at Grace and sang, "I heard a rumor..."

Ah damn. Trepidation bloomed in the pit of her stomach. Carolyn always brought up rumors when her mind started slipping away. "Yeah?" she asked, keeping her voice upbeat. "Was it that I'm going to come bake sugar cookies with you Christmas morning?"

Her mother gasped and grinned. Grace's heart lightened, and she took the moment for what it was—fleeting.

"With sprinkles?" Carolyn asked.

"Every color," Grace confirmed.

"And icing?"

"Vanilla, your favorite."

"Oh, fun." Her mother clapped her hands like an excited little girl. "I can't wait. I can't wait to tell you the newest rumor..."

Carolyn's mind slid from one topic right into another without realizing the shift.

"Not the cookies, huh?" Grace propped her chin in her hand. "Is it..." Grace thought about the other patients in the house and lowered her voice, "that Henrietta and Bob are still getting busy in the shower?"

"Pffft," she said with a frown and a wave of her hand, "that's old news."

"*What?*" Josh asked, clearly scandalized over the suggestion that two of the housemates were often found having sex when left unattended.

Grace shook her head. "Evidently, people in their eighties get quite a bit of action." To her mother, she asked, "What's this rumor that's got you so giddy?"

Carolyn darted a glance toward Josh, then leaned in to Grace and whispered, "I heard...Josh is in love with my Gracie."

Grace's smile froze. Tingles spread outward from her chest and made her almost as giddy as her mother. Though, this was old news as well. She'd known Josh loved her when she'd asked him to come live with her. She'd known he loved her when he'd moved away. And she sure as hell saw the truth of the rumor in his reddening face as he slumped in his chair, wiped a hand down his face, and muttered something that sounded like "Jesus fucking Christ, Carolyn."

Grace bit her lip against the urge to laugh at his distress. And she couldn't resist the urge to make it just a little worse. "That's a great one, Mom. I've got another one for you."

And she leaned forward and whispered in her ear.

Carolyn's face lit up like the Christmas tree in the corner. "Oooooh, that's so... *delicious*."

"Okay," Josh said, resting his head in his hand. "I'll bite. What's the new rumor, Carolyn?"

Carolyn leaned toward Josh this time. His gaze held on Grace, clearly dubious, but he leaned forward when Carolyn gestured him toward her. He was looking at the tabletop when her mother whispered, "I heard...my Gracie loves Josh more."

Pleased with herself, Carolyn giggled. But Josh had frozen in place. And even when she sat straight and started working on another butterfly, Josh remained still, staring at the table. If brains generated steam, it would have been coming out his ears.

For a moment, Grace wondered if he could really be in such deep denial that the quasi declaration had scared him stiff.

Carolyn picked up a butterfly outline and looked at it as if she'd never seen one before. "What's this?"

Then she glanced around the table, becoming visibly jittery. "What's all this? Why is the table such a mess?"

Josh looked up then, confusion in his gaze. He calmly put his hand over hers and pulled the butterfly from her hand. "Just one of my crazy projects, Carolyn. I'll clean it up. I promise."

Tammy stepped up to the table and patted Carolyn's shoulder. ""I'll take her, Josh. I think someone's getting tired. She helped Carolyn to her feet with a "Don't worry about the table, you two. I'll get it. Go on and get some time together now."

Grace pushed to her feet and walked to her mother's side.

She hugged her and kissed her cheek, and brushed her hair back. "Love you, Mom. I'll see you tomorrow."

"Love you too, sweetheart." Her smile shook, but Grace could tell by the look in her mother's eyes that she was lucid again. "He's a good man, Gracie. The man you should have been with from the beginning."

Grace nodded. In hindsight, that was probably true. But that was the past. And even if they did love each other now, that didn't solve the problems standing between them. Love wouldn't vanquish Josh's sense of duty to Isaac. Love couldn't bridge the one-hundred-and-twenty-mile gap between LA and San Diego. And love would certainly never cure Alzheimer's.

She watched Tammy walk her mother toward her bedroom down the hall, thinking about her mother, Isaac, Josh...

"Grace." Josh's voice pulled her gaze. He stood by the front door, hands in his pockets. "Can I talk to you outside?"

She turned toward him, not sure what to make of that serious expression or the stern tone. "That sounds...ominous."

He didn't smile. Just held the front door open for her as she gathered her purse and passed onto the porch.

"I hope you're not going to rake me over the coals for—"

Josh whipped her around and pulled her into his arms, then stepped her back until her spine pressed one wall of the porch.

"Is it true?" he asked, gazing down into her face.

"What?"

"That you love me?"

Her brow pulled. "You're not serious."

"So...what?" he asked, suddenly defensive. "You were playing your mother? Playing me?"

"Why are you being an idiot? We've loved each other for years."

"No, *I've* loved *you* for years. I didn't think—"

"You're going to stand here and tell me you didn't think I

loved you when I asked you to move in with me after your surgery? Don't even. You ran because you *knew* I loved you."

"No." He gripped her face, softened his voice. "I ran because *I* loved *you*. And I knew I couldn't live in the same house with you and not...mess everything up."

"Mess everything up between you and Isaac."

He heaved a long exhale. "I knew your relationship with Beck was going to be rough. SEAL relationships always are. And I knew you deserved someone better. Someone who could give you a real marriage. But I didn't know what a fuckup of a husband he was."

"He did the best he could. I put that behind me a long time ago." She poked his chest. "You're the one who hasn't been able to get over it."

He searched her eyes with thoughts tumbling over each other in his head. Then his thumbs slid across her cheekbones with a tenderness that knotted her belly with want. His lips touched hers, once, twice, three times, before he pulled back and met her eyes again.

"I'm over it, Grace," he said, firm and sure. "Come home with me."

Her belly fluttered with the promise of his words. But she locked that dreamy little girl in her cage. In Grace's world, believing meant losing. And she wasn't ready to go through losing him again. Not now, when she lost her mother on a daily basis.

All she could do was take what he could give in the moment.

She slid her arms around his waist, loving the feel of his muscles beneath her hands. Aching to get him into a bed so she could feel all that hard muscle and smooth, warm skin against hers.

She lifted to her toes, kissed him again, and said, "I'd go home with you even if you weren't over it."

"Oh, I am," he assured her, taking her hand and leading her off the porch to her car. "My place or yours?"

"Your hotel is closer."

"God, I love the way you think." He pushed her against the door of her car, kissed her hard, sweeping his tongue against hers with a sigh. "I love so much about you, it will take me years to point it all out."

She raised her brows. "Years?"

His mouth kicked up in a hot smile. "Maybe even forever."

That cage took a hard hit, rattling until it almost broke open and let that little dreamer free to wreak havoc on Grace's heart. "Forever, huh?"

He pushed a strand of hair behind her ear. "You're a complicated woman."

She sighed and nodded. A little too complicated for her taste. "I'll follow you to the hotel."

He settled her behind the wheel of her Honda, then jogged to his own car and started the engine. God, she was suddenly anxious. Nerves pulsed along her skin, kicked in her heart, steering her mind toward *Forever? Could it work?*

Just as Josh pulled onto the street, Grace's phone rang. With a quick glance around for cops, she answered, "This is Grace."

"Grace! Baby! You answered."

A chill shivered down her spine. "Isaac?"

"Yeah, honey, it's me. Hey, I can't talk long, but I wanted to tell you that we're touching down in San Diego tomorrow. I'll be home for Christmas this year. Isn't that amazing?"

She stopped at a light behind Josh's car, feeling as if she'd skidded into an alternate reality. "That's great. Are you going up to LA to see your family?"

"If I have time, but not until I get a few days with you."

Frustration bubbled to the surface. "Isaac, I'm working. I have plans with my mother. And you're doing it again. You're acting like we're still married. You know that's why I stopped answering your calls to begin with. And I don't appreciate you sending Josh down to check on me."

"Baby, just because we're not married doesn't mean I've stopped caring about you. I miss seeing you. I miss talking to you."

"Listen, Isaac, this isn't a good time—"

"Hold on." He covered the mouthpiece and yelled to someone in the background, "I'll be there in a fucking minute." Then to Grace again, "I've got to go, baby. I'll come find you as soon as my feet hit the ground."

And he disconnected.

Fury whipped up in Grace's chest like a hurricane. "You son of a *bitch*."

She threw her phone across the car. It hit the dash, the passenger's window, and landed on the seat.

Grace gripped the steering wheel with both hands as she and Josh entered the hotel's parking lot.

Isaac was going to ruin everything. If Josh hadn't already told Isaac where she was and what she was doing, Isaac would find her. And as soon as he found her, he'd find Josh. And as soon as Josh was confronted, face-to-face, with his SEAL brother, his *"I'm over it"* would cave. Grace had seen these men turn into different people as soon as they met up. As if they flipped a switch and turned from ordinary guys to warriors. Blood brothers. Lifelines.

And no good SEAL went against a brother.

It had kept Josh from going after her in the first place.

It had sent him running last year.

And it would put a wall between them now.

Josh pulled into a parking spot, and Grace followed with her heart aching. She turned off the engine and sat there a moment, weighing decisions.

If she gave Josh the news tonight, she'd lose her last chance to love him.

And dammit, she deserved him. She deserved to be completely loved for who she was—even if it only lasted one night.

A night she planned on making sure lived in their memories forever.

8

_____

J osh's head swam with plans for their night together, making him hard before he even got to the car to help her out. He both couldn't wait to make love to her and wanted to take it slow, make it last. The realization that she truly loved him turned him inside out.

But the moment he saw her face, his focus on getting her naked slipped. "Hey." He cupped her face and took a better look in her eyes. Oh yeah, something was definitely wrong. "Gracie, we don't have to—"

She wrapped her arms around his neck, pressed her body against his, and kissed him hard. Her hands sank into his hair, and she opened her mouth, searching out his tongue with her own. When they touched, Josh groaned, and his idea of getting naked with her resurfaced instantly.

"I want to," she said between kisses. "I've never wanted anything more."

He pulled back, searching her eyes. Something wasn't right. "What happened between the house and here?"

"I realized how desperately I want you. How long I've

desperately wanted you." And she kissed him again. Her hands slid down his torso and stroked his erection. His cock surged beneath her hand.

"Ah, Jesus." He broke the kiss and grabbed her hand. "Baby, slow down. I want to take our time tonight."

She pulled out of his grasp and snapped open the button on his jeans. "We have all night to go slow."

His zipper went next, and her hand pushed into his jeans. The sensation of flesh on flesh made a groan roll from his throat.

"God, I love the feel of you." She pushed his boxers out of the way just as she had the night before and drew his cock fully into her hand. A stroke, a tug, and Josh was on the edge.

He fisted his hands in the back of her dress. "Jesus, Grace... You make me crazy."

"I'm shooting for insane." And she lowered to her knees.

"Whoa...what...?"

Her mouth closed over the head of his cock and his throat closed around his words. One hand slapped back against her car for balance, the other gripped a handful of her shiny, silky hair. Pleasure sang down his spine, and his back arched, pushing his cock deeper into her mouth. She opened and took him in with a hungry moan. The feel of all that soft, moist heat flooded his body with lust. Light exploded behind his closed eyelids. His brain grappled for traction. But her tongue stroked, her lips sucked, driving him into oblivion.

"Mmmm," she murmured, dragging his length from her mouth. "Damn, that's good."

Way beyond good, but he had to preserve the few words he could manage. "Grace... We're in a...parking lot..."

"It's dark," she said, her hand stroking his wet length.

He brought his other hand away from the car to cup her face. "Let's go inside."

She grinned up at him, and the wicked glint in her eye sprayed gasoline on his fire. "Afraid of getting caught?" She pulled his hand from her hair and closed his fingers around the door handle. "You always did love to play by the rules. Let's check out the dark side..."

She took him deep in one long plunge. Pleasure spiked through his cock, up his back, down his legs.

"Mother *fucker*."

The possibility of being discovered added another thrilling layer to the erotic act, and her delicious hums of pleasure made him realize the taboo of public sex was jazzing her too.

And wasn't that just fucking *blistering* hot?

But he needed more than physical pleasure with her. A lot more.

He released the door and gently eased her head back, drawing his length from her mouth. The sight of his cock sliding between her lips almost tipped him back over the edge. But he gripped her arms and pulled her to her feet.

"Baby..." he said, trying to catch his breath, "talk to me."

Her brows pulled in a little crease and her lower lip pooched out in a maddeningly adorable display of disappointment. "What's with you and talking? You never wanted to talk before."

"Which is why I want to talk now. Not talking before kept us apart."

She swayed into him, kissed his lips, then trailed kisses across his jaw and down his neck. "I really don't want to talk, Josh. All I want you to know..." She tilted her head and started back up the other side of his neck. "Is that no matter what happens, I'll always love you."

A tingle of unease burned along his ribs. He gripped her jaw and drew her gaze to his. "Nothing's going to happen."

"Something always happens."

"Not this time." He wrapped one arm around her shoulder,

yanked his jeans into place with the other, and started toward a side door. But a strange and new insecurity floated inside him now, the sensation of losing her when they'd finally just found each other again.

At his room, he pulled the key card from his wallet and faced the door. Grace slipped her arms around him from behind, pressed her body against his, laid her forehead to the indention of his spine, and just held him.

Josh unlocked the door and held it open with his foot, then turned and wrapped her in his arms. Sliding a hand beneath her hair, he lifted her mouth to his and kissed her as they made their way inside.

"God, I love the way you kiss," he murmured against her lips. "Can't get enough."

"And I love the way you feel." Her fingers slipped beneath the hem of his T-shirt and stroked his belly and chest. "Can't wait to get my hands on that body of yours."

Her hands slipped under his shirt, and her stroke tingled over the skin of his belly like electricity.

"Baby, I let you have control last night." He backed her toward the side of the bed, bent his knees, swept his hands up her thighs, and eased her dress over her hips, then braced one knee on the bed and laid her back. "Tonight, it's my turn."

He pressed one hand between her legs, covering her mound. She sipped a gasp and arched her back.

"Oh, *God...*"

"That's what I'm talkin' about," he murmured, thrumming with the anticipation of making her as crazy as she made him.

He kissed her breastbone where her ribs joined, and continued to create a hot, deliberate path toward her belly button. Her hands threaded into his hair. Her hips lifted into his hand. The beauty of it, of having his Grace beneath him, was almost too much to believe. But all he had to do was open his eyes, see her beautiful body spread out on the bed beneath him, bathed in moonlight spilling through the window, and he knew it was real.

He lifted the other knee to the bed, spread his hands across her flat belly, and let them sweep up, dragging her dress overhead and exposing a lace bra that matched her tiny panties.

Cupping her face between his hands, he kissed her gently. "This will never change, Grace. Me loving you will never change."

Josh kissed a line down the middle of her body until he reached her panties, then opened his mouth over the lace covering her pussy and breathed long and hot. Grace groaned, the sound a languid plea for more. He kissed her through the lace. Licked her. Another soft moan from her throat heated his blood. He spread his hands over her thighs and pressed her legs wide, rubbing his face over her soft pussy. She smelled spicy and sultry and musky. Delicious.

He tugged the lace away from her sweet spot and found her pussy bare. Completely and totally bare.

His cock hitched against his jeans.

"Fucking beautiful," he breathed, then licked, and moaned at the taste of her—sweet, tangy, hot. And licked again. Deeper. "Mmm."

"Oh, shit..." Her hips rocked and wiggled. Her hands fisted in his hair. The sights and sounds of her pleasure turned his blood to jet fuel. He gripped the panties at her hip, and with one pull, the flimsy fabric snapped.

"Oh my God." Grace gasped. "You *ripped* them? Those are expensive."

"Now who's concerned about rules? I'll make it worth your while," he said before covering her pussy with his mouth. And, oh God, yeah, this was what he wanted. Warm, soft, erotic...

"Fuck," she choked out, back arching of the bed. "Oh my God... Josh."

Hearing her scream his name was a wild aphrodisiac. He growled with lust, opened his eyes, and watched her fall back on the bed, arms overhead, fisting her hair. Her head rolled back and forth, her back arched, her hips writhed. And the sounds that scraped from her throat set fire to all that fuel inside him.

"Josh... God... *Please*..."

He knew exactly what she wanted. And he smiled as he eased her folds open, took her clit between his lips, and suckled.

Grace cried out and slapped one hand to the bed, fisting the comforter. "Jesus... Josh..."

Her body bowed, jerked, and tensed. Her head fell back, mouth dropped open, and her thighs clamped around his shoulders as her hips bucked against his mouth.

Her explosion was quick, hot, and intense, and Josh floated on the ecstasy of her pleasure. As the aftermath faded, her body went lax, and her thighs fell open around him.

He rested his chin on her belly, focused on pulling his own body back from the edge while he let her enjoy the postorgasm euphoria.

"Oh my *God*," she breathed, tossing a forearm over her eyes. "You're so *good* at that."

An unexpected chuckle popped from his throat. He buried his face in her belly, which made her laugh too. "Why do you sound so shocked?"

"Because I've never... It's never...been that damn *good*."

His ego soared. His heart swelled. He crawled along her body, stroking the soft skin of her belly, sliding his finger along the edge of her bra, searching for the clasp. He found it between her breasts and flicked it open, spread the fabric, and stroked the perfect flesh.

"You were right." Her comment brought his gaze up to her relaxed, gorgeous face. "That was totally worth the price of new panties."

He leaned down and kissed her, long and slow. "Baby, I will buy you an unending supply of panties if that's what it takes to get my mouth on your sweet pussy."

"If I had the strength, I'd rip your shirt off." She twisted, grabbed the edge of his tee and tugged, barely moving it an inch. "Help me get you naked."

He ducked his head and let her pull his shirt off over his head. She made a purring sound in her throat that did crazy things to Josh's gut. Propping herself up on her side, she pushed his shoulder down and rolled on top of him, then scooted down the bed, grabbing his jeans and boxers and pulled them off his legs at the same time.

"Hold on." He caught his jeans before she tossed them aside, and dug around for his wallet. Then found the condom buried in there.

She took it from him. "That's the best you can do? One?"

He raised his brows with a smirk and a shrug.

She stroked her hands over his body. Her touch created tingles everywhere. Then one hand closed around his cock, and the tingles turned electric, making Josh bow. "Ah, God..."

"This guy looks like he needs some attention." She stroked his length, then lowered her head.

Josh caught her by the jaw before she closed her mouth around him. "Sweetheart, I won't last, and I'd kill to get inside you right now."

"That's fierce." A hot little grin tipped her mouth, and she picked up the condom, sliding her tongue over her lower lip. "I like fierce." Then she narrowed her eyes at the package. "Why does this look like it's been living in your wallet for a year?"

Josh stroked his hands up her sides, cupped and squeezed her breast. "Because it has."

Her head tipped in the most adorable way. "Why?"

"Because one-night stands were easier when you were married, or I was leaving town the next day on an op."

But she wasn't off-limits anymore. And his op days were over.

For the first time in a year, that thought didn't drag him down. He'd found that one woman he could promise tomorrow. Promise next week. Promise next month. He'd found the woman he could promise the rest of his life. And his yearning for those ops and his team vanished.

She tore the package, pulled out the condom, and carefully rolled it on. Josh fought to hold still, clutching her thigh to keep from rolling her to her back and plunging deep between her legs.

She slid one thigh across his hips and stroked the head of his cock over her slick entrance. "You do realize we'll have to go out and get more of these tonight, right?"

He reached up, hooked his hand around the back of her neck, and pulled her down. She braced herself with a hand on his chest, and he kissed her deeply. "I'll do anything you want, Gracie."

"I want you to fill me. Now."

With his hand still around her neck, holding her eyes with his, he gripped her hip and eased her down.

His head pushed past her entrance, snug, warm, soft, wet, and they groaned in unison.

When she met his gaze, her eyes hot and heavy-lidded, he pushed deeper. The pleasure washing her features thrilled him. And when he filled her, he rolled until they'd switched positions and spent long moments kissing and touching her beautiful body while buried deep inside her.

She'd been right all those months ago. They were perfect together.

And as the desire built and they began to move together, driving each other toward the sweet promise of ecstasy, Josh knew this was where he wanted to stay forever.

9

G race put the last clip in Tiffany's updo. "There you go. Just pull this one pin, and your hair will fall everywhere."

"Perfect." She stood and smoothed down the bodice of her corset. "Thanks, Grace."

She glanced at the clock above the dressing table. Almost 6:00 p.m. And still no word from Isaac.

Maybe he wasn't going to show. Maybe he'd talked to Josh. Though Josh hadn't said anything, and his only odd behavior today had been trying to figure out *her* odd behavior.

What a pair.

Grace slipped out a side door and walked around the front of the building to avoid Josh's watchful eye from the studio. He was too perceptive. He noticed the slightest change in her mood, almost seemed to be able to read her thoughts. She'd always thought it would be great to have a man like that—until she was trying to hide something.

Walking in the front door, she caught a what-the-hell look from the bouncer, Theo. "Where'd you come from?"

"Around the side. No sign of him?"

"Nothing."

She drummed her fingers on the podium up front. "The others know?"

"If anyone comes in tonight asking about you, we get ahold of you discreetly. No one goes to Josh even if this Beck guy asks for him."

"Thanks, Theo. There's a big tip in this for you on payoff."

He grinned and saluted. "Anything for you."

"And the almighty dollar."

"Amen."

She sighed, growing more nervous by the moment. "Okay. I guess I'll head back again."

Exiting through the front door, she made her way toward the side entrance again. As soon as she stepped inside, someone slipped a hand around her arm. She startled, twisted, and found Josh.

"Baby, what in the heck is going on with you today?" he asked, clearly concerned.

She exhaled, slipped her arms around his waist, and leaned into him, but not skin to skin like she preferred. He was working without a shirt again, layered in dirt and sweat. She was dressed in white silk, with a long night of customer contact ahead. Under different circumstances, he wouldn't have been able to peel her off him.

"Someone didn't let me get any sleep last night," she said. "I get jittery when I'm tired."

He stroked back a piece of hair off her forehead. "It was the other way around, sugar."

"Speaking of sugar..." She followed the hollow of his throat with the tip of her index finger. "Would you want to come make cookies with me and Mom tomorrow? We've made sugar cookies on Christmas day for as long as I can remember."

He stroked her cheek with the backs of his fingers. "Can I smear you with frosting and lick it off?"

"Afterward, absolutely."

He grinned. "I wouldn't be anywhere else—"

"I want to see Grace." The bellow erupted from the direction of the back door, and Grace recognized Beck's voice immediately. A river of ice slid through her chest. Panic stung her heart. "Grace Beck. I know she's working here."

"Sir, step outside before we take physical action," Theo's voice interjected. "We don't have an employee named Grace."

Josh's hand closed on her arm, drawing her gaze. "Grace," he hissed, "what is he doing here?"

"Get your hands off me, dude," Isaac said. "I don't want to hurt you, but if you touch me again, you're going down."

"Jesus." Grace turned toward the mayhem, but Josh pulled her back, and when she looked at him again, hurt and fury flushed his face.

"Last time I talked to him he was halfway around the world," Josh said. "Grace, what in the fuck…?"

"I'm sorry…" She put a hand to his chest. "Let me go take care of this before someone gets hurt."

He ignored her, searching her face as the facts took shape in his mind. "You knew he was coming." He released her and stepped back but blocked her path. "When? When did you know?""Josh—"

"When?"

Grace jumped at his bark. "He called last night—"

"On the drive to the hotel." Realization filled his voice, and hurt crept into his handsome features.

"You talked to him on the drive from your mom's to the hotel."

More voices joined the fray near the back door. "Please, Josh—"

He gripped her arms, his expression shifting to one of accusation. "Why didn't you tell me?"

"I don't know." She couldn't think. "I...I—"

"You didn't trust me," he finished, his hands tightening. "You knew he was coming, and you thought I'd bail again if I had to face him. You thought I'd choose my loyalty to him over my love for you."

The betrayal in his eyes broke her heart. He was 100 percent right. She'd been 100 percent wrong. She should have trusted him.

"I'm sorry—" she started, interrupted by Isaac's bellow.

"I'm not going anywhere until I find Grace."

"Josh, please let me go before this gets out of hand."

He hesitated, then released her, his expression a mix of fury and pain. She hurried toward the main dressing area and found Isaac blocking the rear door as if he were guarding the president.

"Stop yelling," she ordered.

"WHAT IN THE FUCK, Grace? What are you—" He broke off, his gaze shifting over her shoulder, and by the look in Isaac's dark eyes, she knew Josh had come out. "Marx, what in the fuck are you doing here?

You're supposed to be in Philadelphia."

Grace stepped up to Isaac and pushed him backward. "Let's talk about this outside," she ordered.

"Now."

"You lied to me, you fucker." Isaac stabbed a menacing finger toward Josh. "You told me she wasn't stripping."

"I'm not stripping, Isaac."

"Then why are you dressed like a hooker?"

"Do you hear those sirens, Isaac?" she asked. "Those are

coming for you. And I sure as hell won't be bailing you out. Now take this outside, or I'll let them take you to jail."

Isaac spun on his heel and stalked through the door, shoving Theo aside.

Grace squeezed Theo's forearm and murmured. "I'm so sorry."

"I'll be right here in case you need me."

Josh pointed at Theo. "You're going up front to steer the cops clear. If you don't, things will get extremely ugly. I've got this handled."

Theo's worried gaze darted through the open door.

"Now, dude," Josh demanded. "*Go.*"

When Theo turned and hustled toward the front of the club, Josh slipped off his watch and handed it to Jasmine. "In three minutes— *three*"—he tapped the watch face—"you create some kind of emergency to get Grace inside."

Jasmine nodded. "Got it."

Josh stepped outside, where Beck and Grace stood four feet apart, arguing. Dressed in jeans and a T-shirt, Beck looked almost the same as he had the last time Josh had seen him: tall, chiseled, dark, and sporting a few scrapes and bruises on his face and forearms.

Beck swept a hand up and down, gesturing to Grace's body. "What is this? Who are you? What happened?"

"The same thing that always happens when you're gone, Isaac. Life happens. I grow and change, and you come home the same judgmental asshole."

"Maybe because those changes aren't for the better."

"Says you. But the funny thing is, it's my life. Not yours, not ours, *mine.* Good or bad, they're my changes to make."

"I care about you," Isaac implored in a way Josh knew was true. Beck wasn't a bad guy; he was just dense and self-absorbed. "I want the best for you."

"Then leave me to live my life. You coming here creating drama is *not* best for me."

Beck rubbed his face with both hands, and his gaze landed on Josh. "I trusted you, you fucker."

"I did exactly what you asked. And Grace is perfectly fine. I didn't lie to you."

"Don't fuckin' split hairs with me, asshole. And what the fuck are you still doing here?" He gestured to the tool belt around Josh's waist. "What's that about?"

Josh opened his mouth to answer, but Grace spoke first. "He's helping me build a studio, Isaac. I told you, I'm teaching, not stripping. Josh believes in my abilities. He doesn't try to stuff me into the box of a twenty-two-year-old and keep me there."

Oh...shit... Just as Josh had expected, Beck read between the lines. His body stilled. His gaze darted between Grace and Josh, disbelief and anger mounting in his expression. "Wait... Are you two...?"

Reality hit. His expression turned murderous, and he straightened, hands balled into fists at his side. "Are you *fucking* my wife, asshole?"

Jasmine stepped outside. "Grace, we need you in here. Colleen fell. I think her ankle might be busted."

A sound of shocked agony popped from Grace. Josh jerked his head toward the door. "Go. Beck and I have to work this out."

Grace stiffened and pointed a stern finger at both of them. "I swear to God, if you two start brawling out here, I'm going to make sure you both end up in jail. In the *same cell*."

After Grace disappeared inside, Jasmine closed the door. The snick of a dead bolt gave Josh one tiny sliver of relief— Grace was safe. He, on the other hand, was in a world of trouble.

As expected, Beck came at Josh full speed and rammed his shoulder into Josh's chest, rocketing him back against the building. Before Josh had time to suck air, Beck flattened his hand against Josh's chest and raised his fist.

"Give me one good reason I shouldn't fuckin' beat the shit out of you right now."

Josh looked Beck directly in the eye. "I'll give you two—one, Grace divorced you three goddamned years ago. She's not your wife, she's your *ex*-wife, and she has the right to see anyone she pleases, the way you've seen a dozen different women since then. And two, think about what happened the last time you tried to beat the shit out of me."

Beck's lips thinned. The memory of ending up stuck in the infirmary side by side for three days after they'd gotten in a stupid-ass brawl over an op gone bad flashed in Beck's eyes. He growled and shoved Josh against the building again, but then backed off, pacing in the night.

Josh took a breath, then let all his anger toward the man pour out. "If you cared about Grace the way you just claimed to care, you wouldn't have married her in the first place." He pushed off the wall. "You wouldn't have volunteered for all those extra assignments that kept you overseas." He started a slow progression toward Beck as he spoke. "You would have come home when you could have and given Grace the family she's always wanted. You would have fucking helped her with the expenses of keeping her mother in an Alzheimer's facility when she told you her mother was sick."

Beck stopped pacing, turned on Josh, and yelled, "She didn't want help. I did offer. She kept turning me down."

"That's a fucking copout. That's like saying bin Laden wouldn't come out of hiding, so we just stop trying to find him. Grace was your wife. You know she's stubborn and independent. They're two of the things you loved most about her. And they're the very reason you two stayed married as long as you did. A weaker woman would have bailed on your ass the first time you extended your tour instead of coming home—and she'd have been justified. If you really cared about Grace, you would have pushed through her resistance. You would have found a way to help.

"Because the truth is, she's working at this strip club because *you* didn't step up, shithead. She's doing what she needs to do to pay the crazy bills, because this is her mother we're talking about. A mother who has always treated you like her own son. A mother who's treated you better than your own fucking mother—"

"Okay," Beck yelled, throwing his arms out and pacing again. "Jesus, dude, the horse is fucking dead already."

Josh shut up. Watching Beck pace as he absorbed everything he'd denied until now but had to accept.

And in the silence, Josh had to find his own resolution to the realization that Grace had been right all along—love alone wasn't enough. They also needed trust. And not only hadn't she trusted Josh's commitment to her, but she'd tried to keep Beck's visit a secret.

Now, Josh had to accept the fact that Grace might not be 150 percent committed to their relationship.

And without that, Josh couldn't envision how they could make things work between them.

"Do you love her?" Beck's question yanked Josh back from the painful realization. "I mean *really* love her."

That was an ironic question coming from the self-centered Beck. Then Grace's words came back to him. *"In his own way, he did his best."* And despite the discrepancies between Grace's and Beck's reality, Josh believed that, in his own way, Beck had truly loved Grace.

"Yes," he said for the second time in two days. "I *really* love her. But even if things don't work out with us, you have to let go, dude. Let her find someone who can really give her what she wants and needs."

All the confrontation drained from Beck's muscles. With his gaze locked on the asphalt, he nodded.

"Yeah..." he said, his voice dripping with resignation. "Man... This fuckin' blows."

That was a mild way to put it, but Josh was suddenly experiencing the same sense of loss.

"All right." Beck straightened and pulled himself together the way Josh had seen him do hundreds of times in the field. "There's only one thing left to do, I guess."

Josh wished he knew what to do at this point. He was fucking lost and felt like he was bleeding out.

"Incoming."

Beck's strange warning drew Josh's gaze from the ground a split second before Beck's fist slammed into Josh's face. His head jerked to the side, the pain following as he stumbled and hit a nearby Dumpster.

Pain blasted through his head, burning across his skin and cutting into his eye. Josh braced himself for a second attack.

"You *motherfucker*," he said, squinting toward Beck. When he found his former teammate doing nothing more than standing there, shaking out his hand, Josh relaxed. "That was a cheap shot, you fuckin' ass wipe."

"Believe me, you'll appreciate it," he said. "Grace freaks over every little scrape. You'll get more attention than you know what to do with."

He pulled his hand away and found it covered in blood. "You are such a prick." Josh turned toward the building and knocked on the door. "Jasmine, it's Josh."

"God. Out of commission for a year, and you're a grade-A pussy," Beck muttered.

"I've been out of commission for a year and my priorities are a hundred and eighty degrees different.

Grace has had enough drama for a lifetime," Josh said as Jasmine opened the door. "I'll be right back.

Stay out here so you don't freak the entire club."

"Are you okay?" Jasmine asked, her eyes pulling down at the corners with her frown. "Do you want me to have Theo drive you to the ER?"

"No, no," he said, turning toward the studio and the bathroom alongside. "I'll be right out. He's calmed down. Everything's going to be fine."

But when Josh braced his hands on the counter, watching blood drip, drip, drip into the white sink, he was having serious doubts about Grace's true feelings toward him, and whether or not they could really make this work.

10

Grace secured the ice pack on Colleen's ankle with an ace bandage. "That should keep it from swelling." She glanced up at the young woman who seemed suspiciously nonchalant over an injury that could potentially cripple her dancing career. But she couldn't worry about that now, she had to get outside before two SEALs tried to kill each other. She had to get outside and explain her royal fuck up to Josh and hope, pray he would forgive her, then beg if necessary. "Are you okay?"

"Oh, sure, yeah," she said absently, glancing up from filling her nails. "Much better. Thanks Nikki."

She pushed to her feet and turned to find Jasmine. Grace gave her a suspicious, narrow-eyed gaze. "If this supposed busted ankle ended up getting Josh hurt...I'm coming back for you."

Starting past, Jasmine cried, "But he's the one who told me to do it."

Grace didn't even glance back over her shoulder, just hurried to the back door and stepped out. She was breathing hard when she found Isaac standing twenty feet away, arms crossed, gaze staring off into the distance.

She wandered closer, her gaze scanning the back lot, searching for Josh. But Isaac was alone. A burst of hysteria shattered in her chest. "Where is he?" she demanded, drawing Isaac's gaze, and approaching him so fast, he didn't have time to answer. She slammed her hands against his chest. "Where's Josh? Did you hurt him? Did you chase him off, you son of a bitch?"

Isaac grabbed her wrists. "Hey, hold on-"

She jerked away and fisted her hands at her sides. "All I ever wanted was to be happy, Isaac. I tried so hard to be what you wanted, but I was never enough. I finally find a man who loves me for me, and you can't even let me have that three years later."

She turned her back on him, frantic and lost. Josh's absence left a black hole inside her.

"Take it easy, Grace-"

She swiveled back toward Isaac, Josh's loss stabbing her heart like a knife. "No. I won't take it easy. I love Josh. I've loved him for years, but you've always come between us. He's given you five hundred times the loyalty you deserve, and what have you given him? Heartache. Loneliness. You're as lousy a friend as you were a husband."

"Whoa," he grimaced, taking her hysteria in stride, as if this wasn't life-altering. "That's a little over the top, honey, but I can understand-"

"Goddamnit," she screamed, stomping her foot like a two year old out of sheer frustration. "I'm not letting you ruin this, and I'm not letting him run again. Where did he go? Tell me right fucking now, Isaac, I won't lose him again."

"I'm right here."

Grace gasped at the sound of Josh's calm voice and spun, nearly toppling in her stupid heels. The sight of him, his left eye raw, a cut oozing blood just above his eyebrow turned her anger into concern. "Oh my God, you're bleeding." She walked toward him while yelling at Isaac. "I told you not to hurt each other."

When she got close, she raised her hand to his head, as if the touch would cure him, but he intercepted.

Grace's gaze snapped from the injury to Josh's face as a whole, and her heart dropped to her feet. His eyes were dark, his expression serious.

"I'm fine."

No, he was not fine. He was distant. Closed off.

"And if I want to stay fine," Isaac said, "I think this would be a good time to hit the road." He walked over and pulled Grace into his arms. "I'm sorry, honey. I won't bother you anymore. I really do want you to be happy. I know he'll take care of you."

He released her and held out a fist to Josh. "Call me, dude." Josh met the bump with a tired smile.

"Might want to get some ice on that eye."

Then he rounded the corner of the building and was gone. Grace found herself shaking-with adrenalin, anger, confusion... "What...just happened?"

Josh exhaled, hooked his thumbs in his front pocket and took a few steps toward her. "He gets it. He just needed to hear it from a different perspective."

She exhaled, working up the nerve to look at him, and when she did, when she realized how badly she'd screwed up, her heart broke. "I just...I didn't want to lose you again. I didn't want you to have to choose again."

He shrugged and took another couple steps closer. "You had good reason to doubt me, but its different now, Grace. We're different. If this is going to work, you have to trust me."

If this is going to work...

Hope burned through her heart and tears stung her eyes. Her throat closed around a ball of emotion.

Unable to speak, she nodded emphatically.

Josh slipped his arms around her waist, kissed her forehead and murmured, "Because I'll always, always choose you."

A pent up sob of relief and joy escaped, and she pressed her face to his shoulder. Josh stroked her hair, kissed her temple.

Grace lifted her head, caught another look at his swelling eye and winced.

"From that look, I'm assuming I need ice."

She cupped his cheek. "I have something better."

Pushing up on her tiptoes, she pressed a gentle kiss to the bruise forming around his eye, then tipped her head and kissed his lips. He opened, pulled her closed and kissed her back.

When she pulled away, she stroked his cheek. "Does this mean we're still on for cookies with mom tomorrow?"

A smile lifted his mouth. "Only if the icing rule still applies."

"Actually..." she took his hand and slowly started toward the back door. "I happen to have all the baking supplies in my car. If you'd like, I could give you a little Christmas eve icing demo when we both get done here."

"Mmm," his hum was laced with interest.

Before they entered the club, Josh stopped, turned to her and cupped her face in his hands. "I love you Gracie Nicole. And as long as you want me, I'll be here."

The joy was so complete, it was painful. She leaned in, kissed him, and then whispered, "I love you more."

11

"Jingle bells, jingle bells..." Tammy sang from the table in the kitchen where she sat decorating cookies with Harriet, "Jingle all the way..."

"Oh, what fun it is to have a fresh rumor on a sleigh—" Carolyn cut in as she rolled out sugar cookie dough on a floured board atop the kitchen counter.

Grace laughed and turned the dough. "Somehow, that's not the way I remember the song going."

She'd spent the last few months preparing herself for a failed attempt at their holiday tradition. But, not only had the morning been a grand success, Grace had to admit this might just be the very best Christmas day ever.

"Remember the rule," Tammy said. "No talk of rumors today, Carolyn. Here, Harriet," she set another sugar cookie in front of the older woman, "dress up this reindeer, and let's try..." She started singing,

"Rudolph the red-nosed reindeer..."

A ping sounded through the house, signaling the front door had opened.

Josh's "Just me" mixed with Tammy's, Harriet's, and Carolyn's "Had a very shine-y nose..."

Grace's heart swelled with love and gratitude. She still didn't know how they were going to make a relationship work with the two-hour drive between LA and San Diego, but she'd promised Josh to let go of the worry today.

Josh came around the corner into the kitchen, came up behind Grace, and set the premixed icing on the counter. "I got two." He pressed his body into Grace's from behind, kissed her neck, and whispered, "Just in case."

"Josh," Carolyn said. "I heard a new rumor..."

"Carolyn," Tammy scolded.

Grace turned her head and kissed Josh. "Good thinking." They'd obliterated an entire can the night before in wickedly decadent ways that made her sex tingle with the thought. "Is that what took you so long? Deciding on one can or two?"

"No." He slipped one arm around her waist and set a small box on the counter with his other hand.

"This is what took me so long."

"Oooo," Carolyn said. "That's my rumor. Josh is bringing Grace a special present."

Grace's shoulders went soft, and she smiled at him. "We agreed, no presents."

He shrugged. "I had two of the three before we made that deal."

"Carolyn," Tammy said, standing from the table and taking Grace's mother's arm, "let's go into the living room and open one of your own."

With Harriet on one arm and Carolyn on the other, Tammy exited the kitchen, and silence filled the space.

Grace slipped her arms around his waist. "This is the best Christmas I've had in decades."

"For me too." He combed his fingers through her hair, something that had become a familiar, soothing gesture. "Ready to open?"

She exhaled, feeling guilty she hadn't gotten him anything. But she hadn't had any time. Still, as she picked up the box, small and square, a giddy excitement bubbled in her chest.

She tugged one end of the red bow and slid the ribbon off, then darted a look at his face before she lifted the top. He was smiling but tense. A little edgy.

She lifted the top and found three keys lying on a bed of cotton. Two looked like standard house keys, and one was a decorative, old-fashioned key that looked like a true antique, with a heart at the top of the finger hold.

She smiled up at him. "Okay..." She drew out the word. "Am I supposed to guess?"

"That might take a while, and...yeah," he said, his nervous excitement growing. "I can't wait that long.

Pick a key, and I'll tell you what it's for."

She set the box down, deliberated on the different keys, and finally picked up the simple silver key on the right, holding it up to him.

"Good start," he said. "So, remember when I told you I made a deal with Dean to remodel the back room at the club?"

She lifted her brows. "Yes."

He cleared his throat. "Well, I traded the cost of my labor for a year's lease of the space. The studio is your very own, to use as you choose—for girls at the club, for other dancers to come take lessons, or having your cheerleaders come there. Hell, you can teach pole-dancing fitness to Alzheimer's patients if you want."

That visual made Grace bust out laughing.

"And..." he said, "the payment the girls at Allure make to Dean for your house-mom services now will come straight to you without any cut for a middleman starting January first."

Her mouth hung open. Her heart filled. Her narrow view of

the future opened into a vast array of possibilities. "How did you get him to agree to that?"

"Baby, the man knows you're bringing in clients and money for him hand over fist. Once I convinced him to let me do the renovation instead of giving the job to his alcoholic brother-in-law, the rest was cake."

She stared down at the key. "My own studio?"

"Your very own."

Her heart swelled with more joy than she knew what to do with, and she simply threw herself into his arms, wrapping her arms around his neck and clinging tight. Josh rocked back at the force of her hug and laughed.

"That's the most perfect gift I've ever gotten in my whole life." She pulled back, cupped his face, and kissed him. "I love you so much."

"I love you more." He'd stolen her line, and now they shared it. "Pick another one."

Now, overwhelmed, she turned to the box again. This time she picked up the simple gold key on the left, turned it over and over between her fingers, took a breath, and held it up.

He licked his lips, cleared his throat again, and shifted on his feet. "Okay, so...remember when I found out you were living in that bad part of town, and I was angry that you didn't call me for help? Well," he went on without waiting for her to answer, "that was because I never sold my townhome near yours and Beck's."

"What?"

He shrugged. "The market was down last year, so I held on to it, and I've been renting it out. The couple who'd been living there moved out two months ago, and I've been meaning to get down here and do a few fixes, talk to someone about putting it on the market again, but work's been pulling me in every direction, and I haven't had the time."

A shadow of unease pushed her hand toward him. "I can't take that, and I can't afford—"

He pressed his fingers to her lips. "I'm not giving it to you. At least, not *just* you." He slid his fingers along her lips and leaned in to kiss her. "I want you to live there with me."

She didn't understand what he was saying. "But...you don't live there."

"I do now. There is no way in hell I'm going back to LA. I'm not going anywhere without you, and I know Carolyn belongs right where she is."

"But your work—"

"Can be done anywhere. Yes, I will need to travel. Yes, I may be gone for a few days at a time, occasionally a week, but I've already decided I'm not leaving, Grace, and I want you with me."

She curled her fingers around the key and pulled it to her chest. "Are you sure?"

"Absolutely."

"You don't want to just, I don't know, date for a while and see how it goes first?"

He laughed, head thrown back. "Baby, I know everything I need to know. And I know I don't want to be without you one minute longer than I have to."

"Oh, wow..." she breathed, wide-eyed and choking on emotion. "I've never...I don't..."

He cupped her face, and the nerves returned to his eyes. "I love you, Grace. Please say yes."

He had a way of wiping out all her reservations. "Yes."

He kissed her and wrapped her in his arms, whispering, "That's the best present you could give me."

When he released her again, she picked up the last key and studied it, her memories sliding back to those days of team get-togethers and family visits. "This looks like one of the keys you had mounted in that shadow box hanging in your kitchen."

"Good memory."

"Your grandmother's...or something?"

He nodded.

"This was the key that started her collection. My grandfather gave it to her the day he told her he loved her, explaining it was the key to his heart. And I'm giving it to you as the key to mine."

She couldn't hold back the tears any longer. They spilled over her lashes and tickled her cheeks. Josh pulled something from his pocket and took the key from her. He threaded an antiqued silver chain through the heart, moved behind her, and fastened it around her neck. The key fell directly against her own heart.

He turned her in his arms and traced one finger down the chain with a soft smile. "Perfect."

"I couldn't love you any more than I do right now, Josh Marx." Grace linked her arms around his neck, and pressed her forehead to his. "I promise to take very good care of your heart." She kissed him gently, then whispered, "And that's no rumor."

EPILOGUE

ABOUT THE AUTHOR

Skye Jordan is the *New York Times* and *USA Today* bestselling author of more than thirty novels. She was born and raised in California and has recently been transplanted to Northern Virginia.

She left her challenging career in sonography at UCSF Medical Center to devote herself to writing full time, but still travels overseas on medical missions to teach sonography to physicians. Most recently, she traveled to Ethiopia and Haiti.

Skye and her husband are coming up on their thirty year wedding anniversary and have two beautiful daughters. A lover of learning, Skye enjoys classes of all kinds, from knitting to forensic sculpting. She is an avid rower and spends many wonderful hours on the Potomac with her amazing rowing club.

Make sure you sign up for her newsletter to get the first news of her upcoming releases, giveaways, freebies and more! http://bit.ly/2bGqJhG

You can find Skye online here:
Skye's Starlets | Website | Email

SNEAK PEEK
RELENTLESS (RENEGADES, BOOK #5)

Chapter 1

The smokin'-hot, triple-D gave Troy Jacobs another one of those wicked, I'm-gonna-fuck-you-until-your-eyes-cross grins from across the Venetian's concierge suite. Her attention should have excited him. Should have knocked him out of this damn funk. Should have guided his feet her direction.

But Lifehouse hung in the background singing 'From Where You Are', layering Troy's melancholy mood with and edge that felt more bitter than sweet tonight. He glanced at his watch, and muttered a curse under his breath. He needed to stay and schmooze at least another twenty minutes to make the director happy.

So as Jason Wade sung about distance, wishes, loneliness, and regrets, Troy lowered his gaze to the whiskey in his crystal lowball, resisting the urge to glance out the window for the hundredth time since he'd walked into the suite. A suite with a perfect view of Giselle's gorgeous face crowning the Vegas skyline. He worked to repress the familiar blend of frustration and hurt that created anger. Anger that ate at his soul.

"Got somewhere to be?" Zahara Ellis, a member of Troy's

stunt crew, strolled to his side with that loose, sexy sway of hers, and set her glass of white wine on the window ledge. The scrape she'd earned on the set earlier in the day looked raw against her creamy skin.

"Anywhere but here," he said. "How's that cheek? As soon as you bit the dirt I knew it was going to leave a mark. It's bruising. You've got a very pretty blue halo going."

She lifted her wine glass and pressed it against the scrape. "Feels better with something cold on it."

Lifehouse's subdued tune transitioned into a fun, sexy riff from Nickelback's newest album, 'No Fixed Address', which helped Troy pull his mind from the topic that had been dragging him down for almost a month.

"Was worth it," he told her.

"Easy for you to say."

He grinned, thinking back to the clips they'd come here to watch after a sixteen-hour day. "The dailies rocked."

"Thanks." She grinned, but winced and let the smile fade. Zahara wasn't an official Renegade, but she contracted with the group when they needed a quality all-around stuntwoman. "You're doing great work with Channing. I know you want to be the one doing the stunts, but you're teaching him a lot."

Troy's gaze skipped to Channing Tatum where he was talking with the producer and director across the suite. "He doesn't need much coaching. He's the kind of actor who could put me out of a job."

"Never."

She lowered the glass with a wince. "Casey's going to have to work magic with the makeup tomorrow. And speaking of Casey, I feel obligated to give you a heads up. I overheard she and Becca talking. They've all but got you tied to the bed in your suite, taking turns until none of you can walk in the morning."

He rested his hip against the windowsill and lifted his glass to suck down half the Kentucky Mule floating there, then scanned for the brunette again. Casey had been joined by another dark-haired woman, a production assistant Troy recognized from the set, and now they were *both* giving him the same look.

"Oh, yeah?" he asked, trying to cover for the dive in his mood.

"Oh, yeah." The words dripped innuendo, along with the hint of disgust. "Hey, you deserve to play a little. I haven't seen you with a chick since you got here almost a month ago. But the murky depths of those women's minds scare me."

"Thought nothing scared you."

She hummed around a sip of wine. "It's tough to rattle me, but when they started doling out responsibility for the sexual paraphernalia—lube, cuffs, vibrators, anal beads, nipple clamps, cock cages—I have to admit, it turned dicey. I'm more than a little nervous for you. I think you ought to put 9-1-1 on speed dial in case you need to call in the cavalry." She turned her complex hazel eyes on him. "And, dude, I'm only half kidding."

He purposely tried to engage himself in the idea of a no-strings threesome with the bombshells. Z was right, Troy's schedule had been brutal, but not just for that month. He'd been traveling gig to gig for going on fifteen weeks. He was in desperate need of extracurricular activity, but he was having trouble working up the interest. And the fact that he was still letting Giselle get to him seven years later seriously pissed him off.

"They must not have seen what kind of day we had." Troy tossed back the rest of his bourbon. "Please tell me you're as sore as I am."

"Hell yes." Her soft smile revealed perfect teeth that reflected the strip's glow. "I'm going to make one more round of small talk here, then I'm headed to the hot tub, the masseuse, and bed, in that order."

"Damn that sounds good." He imagined hot water and skilled hands easing his aches and pains. "Why didn't I think of that?"

"Probably because you're too busy thinking about what you've been trying to forget since you got here."

He pulled his gaze from his fellow Renegades stuntmen, Keaton and Duke, where they chatted up a couple of blonde production assistants, and refocused on Zahara. "If that's a riddle, I give up."

Her gaze returned to the window, her focus directly across the strip. She lifted her drink toward the Mirage. "She's really beautiful. So...country fresh, you know? And her voice..." Z shook her head and sighed. "There really are no words. She's absolutely amazing."

Troy's heart took a free fall straight to his stomach. His hands clenched around his glass.

He scanned the people in the room, searching for the leak to his past. Giselle had been long gone by the time Troy had hooked up with the Renegades. Then his mind came around to Rachel, Renegades' former secretary-turned-location scout, who now lived in Virginia with Nathan Ryker, Troy's best friend since childhood and the closest thing he had to a brother. Which meant...

"Fucking Ryker." he rasped. "This is worse than a fucking family with everyone tattling on each other."

"She just wanted me to know so I could watch your back, make sure your head was two-hundred percent into the stunts. Would you rather she told one of the guys?"

"I'd rather she talked to me about it."

"She was going to, but you've been so busy, you two have been playing phone tag. She thought with the demands of the film, an outside perspective might be better. We all need that sometimes."

"That doesn't make it okay." Nothing about his situation with Giselle was okay with him. Not the way they'd broken up. Not the way she'd ignored his calls the first few months after. Sure as hell not the way she still talked to Ryker, but not to him. Never to him. Not one damn word since she'd bailed for the bright lights seven fucking years ago. And he *really* hated the way Ryker seemed to think Troy was still so fucked up that he might screw up a stunt just because he'd seen her goddamned picture. "In fact it's damned insulting."

"Did you know she had the title song for this film before you came?" Zahara asked.

"No." Not that it would have made any difference in his role here, but it would have been nice to know that her face would be splattered over every inch of the strip advertising her *Take Me Home* tour. "Overheard it on set. Ryker could have at least told me."

"I saw her in concert once." Zahara said. "In Nashville when I was working on Days of Thunder. She's an incredible performer. Blew the crowd away."

Pride clashed with residual anger and tangled Troy's chest tight. Where Giselle was concerned, his emotions were as complicated as nuclear physics, as touchy as nitro glycerin, and as potent as TNT.

"Her voice is extraordinary, that's for damn sure," he admitted, his own voice edged with a bitterness he hated but couldn't seem to overcome.

"She's really changing up her image. Transitioning from country to pop. They're calling her the next Taylor Swift."

"Fuck that." Troy laughed at the ludicrous understatement. "They aren't even in the same category. Giselle may sing in the country genre, but her voice would rock rhythm and blues, alternative, soul, jazz, contemporary.

"She's got the vocal dynamics of Mariah Carey and the technical ability of Celine Dion. She's always had a strong voice, but over the years, she's honed it into a fucking powerhouse. And her control..."

He shook his head. "It's just unbelievable. She's got Beyonce's dexterity, flexibility, can lift it to be light and airy or push it to be solid, rich and dark. She's even got a spunky, come-to-Jesus gospel flare she whips out once in a while.

"It all blends with the emotion she puts into every song and marks her work as something really, *really* special. So, no," he shook his head, his gaze locked on the carpet, "Giselle is not the next Taylor Swift. She is way, *way* beyond any level Swift will ever reach."

Troy forced himself to stop. To shut his mouth even though he could go on and on about Giselle's voice and the individual singing and performing talents that made her truly one of a kind. He lifted his glass toward a man in a black uniform and maroon half-apron, who nodded in acknowledgement of his silent request.

When he glanced at Z, her mouth had edged up into a sly little grin. "If you say so, Kanye."

"Ha."

"Where'd a white girl like Giselle get a flare of gospel?"

"One of her foster homes. The mother sang in a Baptist choir, and heard Giselle singing while she was folding laundry. Hauled her to church and signed her up. Giselle said she never did another chore because she spent all her time at choir practice. She would have broken out a lot sooner if her biological mother had left her the hell alone."

"Where'd you grow up?"

"Memphis." The bartender delivered his drink. Troy took the

glass, held his hand up in a silent request for him to wait, and downed the whiskey in one swallow. Grimacing against the burn, he set the glass on the tray with a rough, "Another, please."

Zahara waited until the server was out of earshot before she asked, "All the charity she does is for foster care. Is that how you two met?"

He nodded. "Ryker and I were seventeen when she came to our home."

Z made a soft sound in her throat. "Man, you two got a rough start."

"Rougher for her, a beautiful little white girl raised by addict trash in the arm pit of Tennessee." Giselle had been fourteen at the time, with more scars than any one person should carry in a lifetime. "She's lucky the state took her away before her mother got a chance to sell her for a fix. That's where it was headed."

Z shook her head. "How long were you together?"

Troy took the third drink from the waiter and thanked him, then sipped. "Best friends for two years, lovers for three."

"Wow, long time. And so young. What happened?"

"Nashville." *And my own stupidity*. The memories knifed him in the gut. "Nashville happened."

Z waited for more, but when silence thickened between them, she asked, "And you haven't talked to her since?"

"Nope."

"Long time to be carrying a torch. Why don't you contact her? You know, reconnect? The film is the perfect excuse to start a dialogue."

"I'm not carrying a fucking torch," he lied, scowling at Z. He just hadn't realized how hot it still burned until he'd gotten here. "How would you like it if your ex was plastered all over Vegas while you were trying to work?"

She lifted a shoulder, her gaze going distant. "Mmm, don't know. I've never been that much in love."

"Well, take it from me, no one needs that kind of heartache more than once in a lifetime. Besides, she wouldn't recognize me if we passed on the street. I'm a completely different person now —inside and out."

"Really." Z crossed her arms and narrowed her eyes with a sassy smile, lightening the mood a little. "I was under the impression you were *born* a bad boy."

"Bad, yes. But I was white-trash bad. Not bad-ass bad. And our worlds are light years apart now." He gestured out the window. "Look at her, splashed across the fucking *Mirage* for God's sake." He shook his head and smiled despite the stab of loss. "Man. She really made it."

"So have you," Z said with a little scolding in her voice. "Not too many people can say they've got stupid-ass selfies with just about every Hollywood blockbuster star. Or that the big producers have their numbers programed into speed dial on their phone in case there is some freak problem involving rigging on a set. You're just as famous, just in a lower profile way."

Troy laughed. "There's an oxymoron for you."

"You're not that different," she insisted, serious again. "You're both in entertainment. You're both here. You're both involved in the same movie." She tipped her head with a devilish glint in her eye and lowered her voice. "Don't you wish she could see who and what you've become?"

Only every fucking day.

"Nope. Like I said, rejection isn't my thing." He sought out Becca and Casey and found them watching his conversation with Z. With a single nod, they sauntered toward him. And even the sight of two twelves' on a scale of one-to-ten coming at his beck-and-call left him lukewarm. "*That* is my thing now."

"Oh. My. God." Z's hazel eyes rolled. "You really are *so bad*."

He shot Z a grin. "With absolutely no plans of ever changing.

I believe the *present* is the best way to keep one's mind off the past. And these two lovely ladies," he said, smiling at each as they slid into position on either side of him beneath his outstretched arms, "fit my current needs to absolute perfection. Catch you tomorrow, Z."

Troy guided the women toward the door of the suite, forcing his thoughts off Giselle, off the pain eating at his gut like acid, and redirecting his mind toward the thought of relief through sexual oblivion.

By the time he reached the street with Becca and Casey, the alcohol has softened a few of his rough edges, and the women's attentions temporarily numbed the hurt he'd been living with from his very first sighting of Giselle's photo.

The cool, dry June night air layered a thin film of comfort over him after a very long day working in the caves out in Red Rock Canyon west of town. He didn't even look up at her image as they passed the Mirage, headed toward Troy's favorite sex club in Vegas—an elite, members only place, offering top-shelf pleasure. He'd scored the membership when his boss and former mega Hollywood star, Jax Chamberlin, had gone and fallen in love. A few tugs on a couple of powerful strings had arranged a transfer of Jax's membership to Troy. He would never have been able to meet the who's-who qualification otherwise.

Tonight was free-sex Friday, which meant the main salon would host live sex on-stage. How that differed from the live sex happening everywhere else in the club he didn't know. But it didn't matter because he was way more interested in the whips and chains residing in the Dungeon anyway. Beyond drinking away his angst over Giselle, Troy couldn't think of any other immediate fix for this desolate ache than fucking it away in the roughest manner imaginable. Booze would hinder his performance on set tomorrow. Sex wouldn't. And, lucky for him, the women at his sides had some hard-core predilections for domination and pain with their pleasure. Or so they'd said. Tonight, he'd see for himself.

They slowed as a limo crept along a driveway leading from the back of the Mirage to the street, cutting off the sidewalk path as it waited to turn onto Las Vegas Boulevard.

"Who do you think's in there?" Casey asked.

Becca glanced up to the top of the Mirage. "Ooo, maybe it's Giselle Diamond. She's headlining here."

"Troy," Casey said, her tone hushing as if someone might here them. "Go knock on the window and ask for an autograph."

He barely resisted rolling his eyes. "You two are around movie stars all goddamned day and you still need autographs?"

"She's not a movie star, she's a musician. A singer. My *favorite* singer." Becca turned her pleading brown eyes up to his. "*Please.*"

"She won't open the window for another woman," Casey said, "but she'd open it for a sexy thing like you. Just tell her you're working on the set—"

"No." He didn't mean to bark. He was just so goddamned sick of the way Giselle had been haunting him every god damned minute of every god damned day. She was plastered everywhere —billboards, buses, taxis, elevators. She was always in his head, she crept into his dreams...

One of the limo's rear windows slid down. Casey and Becca gasped in stereo, and Troy's gut burned with apprehension.

The rowdy shriek of several women from inside the car pierced Troy's bubble of unease. Three of the limo's occupants popped their heads out the sunroof, one of which held a champagne flute and wore a plastic tiara adorned with fake jewels.

"Hey, handsome," one of the beauties called from the roof. "We've got a bachelorette party going on here. Want to be the beautiful bride's last hoorah?"

Laughter bubbled from the limo, and Troy's mouth curved.

To his surprise, his mood lightened. Maybe a night hanging with a bunch of happy, drunk, celebrating chicks was more of what he needed after all. He wasn't lecherous enough to touch the bride-to-be, but there were a handful of other hotties in there.

Before he had a chance to say anything, Becca tugged him toward the rear of the vehicle so they could pass. "Sorry, ladies, we found him first."

They fell into step with the crowd again. "Sure you don't want me to check closer?" Troy teased. "Diamond might be hiding in there among all those women somewhere."

"You're too handsome for your own good," Becca said in a half-pout, "you know that?"

He just chuckled. In fact, he did know, but only because he hadn't been all that attractive in his youth. He'd been skinny, struggled with acne, and worn the male equivalent of a perpetual bitch face. So the frequency of women's attentions over the last four or five years continued to both surprise, flatter and amuse him. And for the last few weeks, he'd have to take any flicker of amusement he could get. Now, he found solace in the fact that his role in the film was almost over. He could move onto the next project where Giselle wouldn't push her way into his every waking moment.

A woman emerged from the shadows of the alley, turned toward the strip, and fell into step with the crowd. The fact that she was alone in a sea of couples and groups caught Troy's attention first, but her hair was what held it—a spill of fat, golden curls to the middle of her back. A deep, shiny gold. Not blonde, not wheat, not red. A true, rich gold. The rare but natural color of Giselle's hair.

The woman was alone, dressed in black, wearing a felt hat, and walking with purpose. She'd come from the direction of the Mirage's rear entrance, where all the loading docks and back-stage doors lived.

He cut off the little *"Is that...?"* floating through his mind before it could invade his common sense, and tried to smother the tingle of awareness burning in his belly by reminding himself he would *not* run into Giselle on the strip in a city of over half a million people. The color of the woman's hair probably had more to do with the Vegas lights than reality. Besides, she'd never go anywhere in this insane city alone. She was too famous, too recognizable, and her show that night had ended barely an hour before. She'd be soothing her strained vocal chords with a steam bath in one of the Mirage's penthouses right about now, with a staff of thirty to fulfill her every need. Probably had a handful of boy toys fanning her with fucking palm leaves.

The sidewalks were packed. People moved in two main swarms, one in each direction, a standard crowd for a Vegas Friday night. But Troy couldn't let his gaze pull from those curls bouncing gently against the woman's back...

Stop.

This was becoming a real fucking problem.

Troy purposely slowed his step, letting Goldilocks drift into the sea of people ahead and disappear. And without that little spark of hope, his chest went dark again.

Casey and Becca paused in front of the Bellagio to watch the water show, but Troy couldn't stand still, so he paced along the edge of the crowd.

When he found himself at the alley leading to the club, he peered down the dark, quiet walk. The unmarked purple door was illuminated by a single light and guarded by one big man in a simple tan suit.

The promise of oblivion made Troy's mouth water like a Pavlovian dog.

He turned, searching the crowd for Becca and Casey, but the body count was too high. So he continued toward the club, head down, wondering just what it would take to get Giselle out of his head. Out of his heart. When would he finally be able to put her behind him?

He paused at the discreet entrance and displayed his ID.

"Welcome, Sir." The man pulled a royal blue satin half-mask from his pocket. "Enjoy your night."

"I have two guests," Troy said, taking the mask. "They stopped for the water show next door. Brunettes. Their names are Becca and Casey."

"I understand." He gave a single nod. "Please, stay near the lobby so you can identify them when they arrive."

Troy agreed, secured the mask, and entered Rendezvous. He lingered in the lobby, waiting for the ladies. The seating areas of the main salon were crowded, but not full. From where he stood, he couldn't see any more than various corridors leading to other areas of the club, spaces designed to suit a variety of fetishes and fantasies.

Rhianna's voice pumped out 'S&M', and the rich sounds pulsed through Troy's body, releasing a little stress. He wandered into the large room holding the main stage, and took in the act playing out there, a live display of erotic dominance. But his gaze glazed over the edgy scene of a woman on her knees, the man standing behind her gripping the end of a leather strap looped around the woman's throat.

He wondered if Z was right. If seeing Giselle now might help him finally let go. Maybe seeing how she'd changed, seeing how completely she'd sold out for fame, would kill his romantic memories. Maybe showing her how well he'd done for himself despite her abandonment would give him that elusive power to cut the last lingering tie she held on his heart.

Getting ahold of her would be tricky, not to mention awkward...

The smack of flesh sizzled through Troy's body and focused

his gaze on the stage again. Intricately placed spotlights cast the performing couple in dramatic, almost artistic, shadows. The man brandished a crop whip in his free hand and brought it down for a swift crack on the woman's bare ass. Her cry of pained-pleasure flooded Troy's groin with heat. He was already half-hard.

Lil Wayne's 'Pussy Monster' rocked the room as Troy let his gaze roam the woman's body, curvy and luscious and partially naked. Some type of costume that had been pulled down to expose her tits and pushed up to show her ass. Another set of roving lights titillated the audience with flashes of the performers bodies and gleamed off her spiked heels.

He scanned the space, filled mostly by couples and groups lounging to watch or engage in foreplay before they took their activities into another room. The sight of attractive couples, semi-naked, touching and kissing added blood to Troy's cock, turning it rock hard. He was definitely overdue for a night of mindless, rabid fucking.

"Sir," the bouncer whispered to him from the door. "You're guests are here."

Troy returned to the front, where he vouched for the women who had donned purple masks, marking them as guests, not members.

"Where should we start?" Becca asked, giddy.

"Let's see what's going on in the other rooms before we decide," Casey said.

When she tugged on Troy's arm, he stayed put. "You two check it out and report back. I'll be..."

His words evaporate as two women emerged from a corridor that led to Champagne Court, an upper-crust sex playroom with plush lounges, soft lighting and, pretty much anything pleasurable money could buy—from toys to drugs to sexual services.

Goldilocks. The woman from the street strolled out beside

one of the club's guides, someone who gave newcomers a tour and explained the rules and prices that accompanied special services. Goldie wore a crimson mask, the color of a prospective member, which meant she'd passed the rich and famous requirement. Troy's mind immediately twisted back to Giselle, and nerve endings fizzled hot in his belly.

And *goddamnit*, he hated how this relentless hope of seeing Giselle kept tipping his brain off-axis.

"Hel-lo..." Becca waved a hand in front of his face. "Are you with us?"

"Sure," he refocused on the women. "Go ahead. I'll be right here."

They shrugged and disappeared down the hallway leading to the Dungeon.

Troy scanned Goldilocks from the tips of her shiny black rhinestoned spikes to the top of her golden head. She wore a trendy black leather trench that hit her just above the knees, and now held her hat in the tight curl of one creamy fist. And damn those masks. They did an excellent job of hiding a person's identity. It covered her face from her hairline to her nose, curving down to hide most of her cheek. There was really nothing but the woman's hair color to link her to Giselle. Well, that and her size, a smallish five foot three, maybe one hundred and ten pounds. Yet her mere presence made Troy's gut turn summersaults.

His mind spiraled and spiraled, first convincing himself the woman was Giselle, then assuring himself she wasn't. Couldn't be. Giselle wouldn't be caught dead in a sex club. And never alone.

The guide tucked one hand intimately into the crook of Goldie's arm, head bent close to speak quietly. As the women inched closer to Troy on their way toward the main salon, the guide said something that pulled Goldie's gaze from the partial view of the stage through the arched opening; action now drawing deep moans, and pleasure-drenched mewls. Goldie glanced toward the guide with a little smile on her lips, but instead of meeting the guide's eyes, her gaze slid past the other woman to Troy. And locked on.

He felt the punch of excitement at the center of his chest. Tingles spiraled through his torso, raced down his spine. And his mind toggled like a pendulum.

Yes, it's her.

No, it's not.

With her eyes on his, her smile grew. A tentative, nervous smile. And a tiny dimple created a sweet little divot just outside her lips on the left.

Everything inside Troy froze and heated, stalled and raced— his heart, his lungs, his mind.

That dimple confirmed it—this *was* Giselle.

Every muscle in his body pulled taut, poised to act—to do what, he had no idea, because for the first time in over half a decade, since he'd pulled his shit together after she'd walked away, Troy didn't know what to do or say or think. He couldn't make sense of her presence, still half-questioning his own sanity.

The instant recognition he'd expected to see in her eyes never came. She scanned his face, curious, maybe intrigued, then let her gaze slide down his body in a slow search, as if she were trying to place him. But when her attention returned to his face, her expression had shifted in a way Troy could only label as...distant? Disappointed? Aloof? He didn't know. All he knew was she didn't recognize him. All he new was she turned away.

The grip on his heart tightened.

Yes, he'd changed. Yes, between his mask and his beard, his face was pretty much fully covered. But that didn't stem the pain. It didn't keep the knife from driving into his heart, or the irrational insecurity from the past rushing back. In fact, those torturous months of transition at the end of their relationship, when Giselle had risen from unknown wannabe to golden child, flooded back into Troy's head and heart as if it had been seven days ago, not seven years. And he felt the pain of his humiliation at the hands of her new groupies with the strength of a sledge-hammer to the chest. He'd been downgraded from her best friend to a leech, from her lover to her lesser half, from her strongest supporter for years to her greatest weakness in a matter of months.

And now, even she didn't recognize him.

The guide settled Giselle into a small table toward the back of the room along the far edge of the stage. She faced the door, but didn't look at Troy again, and his insides smoldered with irrational hurt and anger. All his issues, issues he'd fought to put behind him, resurfaced, instantly transforming him from a strong, capable grown man to an angry, abandoned asshole.

The guide exited the salon, and Troy stepped into her path, but kept his voice soft when he asked, "Is she alone?"

Her wide dark eyes appraised him before answering. "She is, but she's observing tonight. Prefers to get the feel before she jumps in."

"Thank you." He refocused on Giselle and found her watching him. Their gazes clicked and fireworks lit off in his gut. But her gaze cut toward the stage, as if she didn't want to get caught looking. Which begged the question—*did* she recognize him after all?

She sat straight, legs neatly crossed, hands resting in her lap. In the midst of a relaxed, sexually open crowd, she looked uptight and out of place. Troy's mind spun and spun, trying to figure out why she'd be in a place like this if she didn't want to be. Or why she was so tense if she wanted to be here. And why in the hell had she come alone? A beauty like her in a place like this...alone? That was just a traumatic experience waiting to happen. One more scar a woman like Giselle didn't need.

He caught his train of thought and a burst of anger heated his chest. What *in the fuck* did he care? She was not his concern. She didn't even deserve his concern. For all he knew, this was some sexual fantasy she was playing out with a guy already here in the club. Or she was waiting for someone to come in. Or...fuck, *it didn't matter*.

A man approached her, lowered to a crouch, smiled, shook her hand. She responded in a perfectly appropriate way—with a smile, a shake, small talk. And a rejection. All very tense, uptight, and rigid.

Troy rubbed a hand across his mouth and turned his back on the salon. He wasn't going to be able to stay now. He wasn't going to be able to engage with anyone else tonight. Maybe not for weeks. Or months. And goddammit, that just fucking sucked. He was *still* so seriously screwed up.

Becca and Casey returned, and in the process of wrapping their arms around him and rubbing their bodies along his, turned him partially toward the salon again.

"Ready to get it on, handsome?" Casey purred.

"Let's head straight to Ecstasy," was Becca's suggestion, referencing one of the free-for-all sex rooms where one could purchase the drug of the same name.

Troy glanced at Giselle again. He caught her watching him just before she cut her gaze away then scraped her bottom lip between her teeth.

The very real possibility that she recognized him and was ignoring him snapped his very last thread of human decency. If he were normal, if he were mature, if he were everything he should be, he'd simply confront her. But he wasn't. He'd never been. And even though his logical mind knew he should walk away, even though his logical mind knew nothing could come of watching her here but pain, bad feelings, and disappointment, his heart...or his emotions...or his psyche...*something*...was festering deep inside. It was as if seeing her had tripped a self-destructive switch inside him. As if it was just a matter of time before the fuse burned out, reaching the explosive, and Troy imploded.

And in some sick and screwed up way, Troy looked forward to it. He relished the anticipation of submerging in the pain that was all he had left of Giselle.

Swinging both arms around the girls' shoulders, he sauntered toward the salon. "Let's warm up in here first."

BLURB

RELENTLESS (RENEGADES, BOOK #5)

Bad boy Troy Jacobs is all about taking risks. As a stunt double for Hollywood's A-listers, there's no fall he won't attempt. With one exception—women. Troy fell hard once, and it nearly broke him. Since then, he's vowed never to trust like that again and he's got everything under control. Until the woman who shattered his heart years before shows up on his movie-set. Country music star Giselle "Ellie" Diamond learned long ago that sometimes love isn't enough. When love got in the way of her goals, she made the tough choice to let go of happily ever after and chased the glitz and glamour of the stage. It may not be all she expected, but now it's all she has. And with a worldwide tour on the line, Ellie needs one last gig to rocket her toward stardom: a high-profile roll in a blockbuster film. Passion sparks, and old feelings return. But while Troy and Ellie grow closer their problems from the past simmer in the background. And this time around, there's more tearing them apart than just one star-studded career. All books in the Renegades series may be read as stand alone books.

ALSO BY SKYE JORDAN

FORGED IN FIRE

Flashpoint

Smoke and Mirrors

Playing with Fire

WILDFIRE LAKE SERIES

In Too Deep

Going Under

Swept Away

THE WRIGHTS SERIES

So Wright

Damn Wright

Must be Wright

MANHUNTERS SERIES

Grave Secrets

No Remorse

RENEGADES SERIES:

Reckless

Rebel

Ricochet

Rumor

Relentless

Rendezvous

Riptide

Rapture

Risk

Ruin

Rescue (Coming Soon)

Roulette (Coming Soon)

QUICK & DIRTY COLLECTION:

Dirtiest Little Secret

WILDWOOD SERIES:

Forbidden Fling

Wild Kisses

ROUGH RIDERS HOCKEY SERIES:

Quick Trick

Hot Puck

Dirty Score

Wild Zone

COVERT AFFAIRS SERIES:

Intimate Enemies

First Temptation

Sinful Deception

Keep up to date on all my new releases by signing up for my newsletter here:

http://bit.ly/2bGqJhG

Get an inside view of upcoming books and exclusive giveaways by joining my reader group here:

https://www.facebook.com/groups/877103352359204/

Made in the USA
Monee, IL
10 September 2023

42482456R00099